# A SAFE SPACE

A NOVEL BY JEFFREY JAY LEVIN

FOR THE BOYS

# CONTENTS

# PART ONE

# THE KIDS

# CHAPTER 1
# THERE'S NOTHING LIKE
# SUMMER VACATION

I may not remember much these days, but I remember that as if it were yesterday. Yeah, as if it were yesterday…

•••

It was one of those days in Chicago that kids prayed for. The sun was out and not a cloud to be seen. You could just bathe in the warmth, no SPF required. Summer vacation and nothing to do but hang out with friends. The year was 1970, and I was the ripe old age of ten. I'd finished my Coco Krispies, being sure to drink up the sweet deliciousness left at the bottom of the bowl when the crunchies were gone. It was 9:30 in the morning, and the house was unusually quiet. I searched for my mother and found her sitting in front of the television set, *As The World Turns*, keeping her enthralled. Next to the ashtray, a half-empty bottle of vodka. I guess it was a way to lose herself in the misery of others while trying to forget the misery that inhabited her waking hours, and, most likely, the hours in which she wasn't awake. Smoke from her Chesterfield curled up from the ashtray and hung in the air.

"Hi, Mom."

She forced her gaze away from the television and

acknowledged me with a half-smile. Reaching for her cigarette, she said, "Hi, Honey." Immediately, her gaze returned to the drama unfolding in the fictional town of Oakdale, Illinois.

"I'm going out," I informed her.

"Have fun," she responded, never looking up.

As much as I was glad to not have to explain my every move, part of me missed having somebody care. I'd gotten used to the new standard at home. Ever since my older brother died two years ago, this was the norm. My father had been long gone by this point. Some days were better, some worse.

Ralphie, my brother, was two years older than me. A couple of kids had been scavenging along the banks of the river, searching for treasure. Instead, they'd found his body, not a mark on him. It was as if he'd decided he didn't need it anymore and planned on roaming free, unburdened of flesh and bone. Nobody had ever explained what happened or how he had gotten to that location.

I missed him every day.

●●●

I retrieved my bike from the shed in the backyard and threw my leg over the seat. It was a black sixteen-inch, three-speed Ranger, the first new bike I'd ever owned. It was my ticket to mobility. To freedom.

If there were such a thing as a bicycle helmet then, I'd never heard of it. Longer hair was the style, and I'd let mine start to grow. As I pedaled down Fargo Avenue, the sun warming my flesh and the wind rustling my hair, I had to smile. Unburdened by adult concerns and not having any form of instant communication due to the lack of technology, I occupied what had to be the sweet spot of life.

What adventure would today bring?

●●●

Fargo Avenue was more than just a street. It was a connector. A thread of asphalt that served as a physical reminder of the spiritual bond between me and my two best friends, Pete Wilson and Mike Plotkin. By the way, I'm Jack. Jack Winterhaven.

The three of us lived on Fargo, separated by six blocks of single-family homes. The routine, even during the school year, was that I, who lived the furthest west, would head east for three blocks to Pete's. Then, the two of us would continue heading east for another three blocks where we'd grab Mike. From there it would be off to school, or, in the summer, to "The Park."

"The Park" was Rogers Park. It was where our elementary school was located and took up over twenty acres of prime City of Chicago real estate.

It was the center of our universe. Everything started at The Park. No matter what we were doing or where we planned on going, it all began at The Park. On weekends during the school year, and almost any time of the day in the summer, it was teeming with people. Young people. The mix included those of us in elementary school, high schoolers, and even some college kids who weren't fortunate enough to go away to school.

Like most city parks, this one had a playground with the typical playground equipment, but also a sandbox with oversized cement turtles. More than one kid had their first kiss under one of those turtles. There were also tennis courts, baseball fields, small round concrete basketball courts, and large expanses of open green space. People used that green space for everything from pickup football games to ice hockey in the winter. Anything we could possibly want to do could be done at The Park.

It was great to have such a safe space.

●●●

"So," said Pete, "what should we get up to today?"

We swayed lazily on the swings, our feet tracing slow arcs through the mix of mulch and dirt that acted as the "soft" surface of the day.

"We could ride over to the beach," suggested Mike. "It's going to be a hot one today."

The beach was about a forty-five-minute bike ride from The Park.

"Damn, I wish I could, but I told my mom I'd be back in

time to help her push the grocery cart home from the store. It's too heavy for her." Pete stared at the ground, tracing circles in the mulch/dirt with his feet. "My dad used to do it with her, you know?"

"We know, Pete," Mike and I said in unison.

Pete's father had died seven months ago. He'd been overweight and chain-smoked unfiltered cigarettes. While carrying a window air conditioner, his heart exploded, killing him instantly. The air conditioner barely survived. Since then, Pete had been the "man of the house," and his mother depended more and more on him for help. I'm not certain she really needed help all the time, but it sure kept Pete around the house.

Mike, who had been watching a couple of teenage girls play tennis, saw some of our schoolmates riding into the park. They had a couple of bats and a sixteen-inch Clincher, which, when new, is the hard-as-a-rock ball that passed as a "softball" in Chicago. "It looks like they're getting a ballgame together," he said. "Wanna see if we can play?"

I looked at Pete to make sure he was OK. He nodded, and I said, "Sure. I haven't broken any fingers in a while. Let's do it."

●●●

It was a fun game. Nobody really cared who won or lost. Well, almost nobody. Ricky, one of our more competitive classmates, was very upset Lonny hadn't run out a ground ball, which, Ricky claimed, cost them the game. By the time everybody had finished mocking Ricky for the way he treated Lonny, the storm had cleared and there were sunny dispositions once again.

●●●

It was almost 1:00 p.m. and we were starving. With no words required, we mounted our metal steeds and headed for The Hot Dog Shack. It was exactly what the name implied. A metal shack which, we later came to learn, was actually an old Airstream trailer that had been converted to its current use. It must have been a cheap find, based on the condition of the exterior. We didn't care. The hot dogs were magnificent, the poppyseed buns squishy, and the greasy fries that filled the brown paper bag, delicious. All for under a buck.

The seating was outdoors, with weathered wooden picnic tables scattered around. When we arrived, we had the place to ourselves—quiet and still. Then a car full of high school kids pulled up, shattering the calm. Based on the way he parked, it seemed the driver had received his license fifteen minutes before getting to The Shack. When they opened the car doors, clouds of pot smoke billowed out, enough to make us cough, which they found hilarious.

"Don't breathe that in too much, little boys. You never know what it'll lead to," one of the laughing former car occupants could barely mutter. Behind him, a familiar-looking mean kid stepped forward and peered at us.

"Be careful, boys," he said to the rest of his cohorts. "I believe this here is the trio of death."

Mike looked at him with a depth of hatred I'd not seen before. "Yeah, and if you don't leave us the fuck alone, we'll be sure that our friend the Grim Reaper visits you real soon."

Mike's older brother, Zach, had a reputation for being a little violent and more than a little crazy. At an even five feet tall, with flaming red hair, Mike was a large, intimidating-looking ten-year-old, so could leverage his brother's reputation when he needed to. This was one of those times. It came in handy for me and Pete, too. I was a pretty average-sized ten-year-old at four feet five inches tall, with mousy brown hair. Pete was the smallest of us, at four feet two inches tall, with jet-black hair. Mike acted as our de facto bodyguard.

They were high enough that they weren't sure what to make of that statement, and being familiar with Zach, they nervously laughed it off and went inside The Shack.

"Hey, you all right?" I asked Mike.

He just stared at his fries and said, "Yeah, sure."

Two months ago, a car accident on the Edens Expressway claimed Mike's mother's life. It was still pretty fresh for him, and he, his brother, and his father were having a tough time. Pete and I took it upon ourselves to make sure he had a good summer. At least as good as it could be under the circumstances.

So, there we were. Three kids with chunks of their souls torn out trying to be as normal as possible.

The circumstances sure sucked.

# CHAPTER 2
# THE RIDE TO PETE'S HOUSE

The encounter with the mean-spirited teen had dampened all our moods. The weather was still warm and the sun still felt good, but none of that seemed to help. Until that point in the day, we'd done a pretty good job of pretending we were whole.

We rode back to The Park and convened under one of the turtles, our bikes forming a barrier on the surrounding ground.

"What an asshole," Pete said, stating the obvious.

"Yeah, like we had something to do with the deaths in our families," I contributed. "Like that's our idea of a good time."

I glanced at Mike. He hadn't said a word since the encounter, and faint streaks of tears still marked his cheeks. I reached out and gave his shoulder a gentle squeeze, but he didn't react.

Without looking at either of us, he said, "So, why us? What did we do? It's just not fair." He was too distraught to even punch the sand in frustration.

"I've had the same thoughts," I said. "And no, it's not fair. At least that's what all my relatives tell me."

"Yeah, mine too," Pete said. "Like that helps."

Silence set in until Mike said, "Jack, it's been the longest for you. Does it get better?"

I had to take a deep breath before answering, stifling the sobs that threatened to escape. "Yes, and no," I was finally able to get out. "Sometimes I forget about my grief, like today, at least for a little while. But then something'll happen and it just comes rushing back. If it's not that a-hole at The Shack, it'll be something else. Sometimes all I have to do is walk by Ralphie's room. Once I think about him never being in there again, it's like the day I found out he'd died all over."

The look on Mike's face was enough to tear my heart open.

"I wish I had a better answer for you, Mike. I really do," I said.

"Yeah," Pete said, "I know exactly how you feel. I'll come home and sometimes I still expect to see my dad sitting in his chair, his burning cigarette in the ashtray on the table. If my mom's there when it happens, I have to sneak off to my room, so she doesn't see me crying. That only makes it worse for her."

Into the hanging silence, Mike said, "Thanks for being honest, guys. It helps to know I'm not the only one."

"Oh, crap!" Pete had just checked his watch and discovered he was late to meet his mom. "I gotta go!"

Not wanting Pete to leave on his own, we scrambled out

from under the turtle, grabbed our bikes, and pedaled like crazy.

•••

We wanted to use the fastest route, so instead of using the paved pathways to get to the street, we rode across the open green space. It was bumpy, with patches of dry dirt making portions slippery. We were riding three abreast, each one trying to ride faster than the other two while not crashing. The wind was rushing through my hair and I felt what it must have been like to fly in an open cockpit bi-plane. We were soaring on the ground. It was glorious and I couldn't have been happier! The look on my companions' faces told me they felt the same.

We were neck and neck and neck in what would have been a photo finish at Churchill Downs. The blacktop beyond the grass was visible, and I imagined that demarcation as being the finish line.

We stood in unison and pedaled with all our strength, yet we remained even. Around fifty yards from the finish line, I prepared for a final push when…

•••

That's where my memory of that "yesterday" ended.

Nothing.

Blank.

A void overflowing with emptiness.

# CHAPTER 3
# THE AFTERMATH

The next thing I remembered was my eyes popping open and seeing a bright white haze. It was like emerging from a cave after spending a week without light. I snapped them shut. Slowly, I reopened them, one at a time, taking in my surroundings.

The brightness was caused by the harsh fluorescent light bouncing off the white paint covering every surface of the room. I was the only occupant, surrounded by machines making all kinds of beeping, hissing, and popping noises. One wall was glass, through which I could see white uniformed women scurrying in the hallway.

A hospital.

I expected, hoped really, to see my mother waiting anxiously at my bedside. The only chair in the room sat against a wall, conspicuously empty.

"Hello," I croaked out to the room, my mouth being desert dry.

A moment later, the door flew open and a young girl not much older than me came to a skidding halt as she saw me in the bed, awake. She wore a red and white striped pinafore.

"You're awake."

"Yes, I am."

She stared at me as if she expected me to dematerialize. When I didn't, she said, "I'll get a nurse," and disappeared into the hall.

●●●

The nurse checked my vital signs and looked at my eyes with a really bright light. After she jotted notes on my chart, she asked me some questions: What was my name? What city did I live in? What day was it? I was two for three, which would have been great had this been baseball. Unfortunately, it wasn't. I was three days off in my last answer.

●●●

Someone from the hospital must have called my mom because she showed up about an hour later, accompanied by my uncle. I saw her eyes were bloodshot, although from crying or alcohol, I couldn't tell. It was probably a combination.

"Oh, honey, how are you?" It sounded more like pleading than the question it was meant to be. My uncle moved the chair to my bedside, and she quickly sat, leaning forward to kiss my forehead. I could smell the alcohol coming off her in waves.

My uncle Jim approached from the other side of the bed and put his hand on my shoulder, gently squeezing in acknowledgment of my mother's condition. When she was too impaired to drive, my uncle often acted as her chauffeur.

"I feel OK," I replied. "Why am I here?"

Jim answered, forcing me to turn and face him. "Jack, you were missing for three days. Your friends Pete and Mike, too."

"What do you mean, missing? We were at The Park, riding to Pete's house."

"And then what?" he prodded.

I thought hard but had no answer. "I don't know. Then I woke up here, in the hospital."

"You can't remember anything?"

"No." I looked at both him and my mother. "What happened?"

"Nobody knows," he finally said.

My mind was racing as I became scared. "What about Pete and Mike? Are they in the hospital, too? Are they OK? Can they remember anything?"

"They're both here, too. They seem to have awoken at about the same time you did. And neither of them remembers anything either."

I squeezed my eyes shut, willing myself to recall something about the missing time. Anything.

Failure.

The door opened, and a doctor came into the room, ambling

toward the bed as he reviewed my chart.

"Well, Jack. Nice to have you back with us. How are you feeling?"

"OK, I guess," I answered.

"Good to hear." Turning his attention to the adults in the room, he said, "Mrs. Winterhaven, now that Jack's awake, I need to run some more tests. It shouldn't take more than an hour or so if you want to wait."

My uncle assessed my mother's condition and said, "I think I'll get Mrs. Winterhaven home. She needs some rest. Come on Karla."

My mother, who had been resting her head on the bed, looked up and muttered, "OK, Jim." When she stood up, she bent to kiss my forehead again and stopped before completing the task. Instead, she reached out and touched the top of my head, a strange look overtaking her face. "Jack, what happened to your hair?"

"What do you mean?" I said, reaching up to touch my head where she had. It felt normal.

She dug through her purse and came out with her powder make-up compact. She opened it, revealing the mirror, and held it so the top of my head was visible to me. Stunned, I reached up and touched the pure white streak—about an inch wide—running the entire length of my head. It unsettled me in a way I couldn't put into words. I turned to her, speechless, my hand still frozen in place.

The doctor, witnessing the encounter, said, "Was this streak not there before?"

Both my mother and I shook our heads and I squeaked out, "No."

"Hmm. Interesting," commented the doctor. "I'll keep that in mind. Now, we really need to get moving. They're holding the CT scanner for us."

Uncle Jim patted my shoulder and said, "OK, doc. Take care, Jack. I'll look after your mother. This has been very hard on her."

●●●

"Oh, man. What happened to us?" asked Pete.

They had given us the green light to get out of bed and walk around, so we met in my room.

"Can either of you remember *anything* about those three days?" I said.

Pete and Mike just shook their heads.

Pete asked, "I wish somebody would talk to us. Has anybody mentioned how or where we were found?"

Mike said, "I heard my father talking to someone about that. He said we were all in The Park lying in the grass just before the blacktop started. According to him, it was as if we, and our bikes, had been spit out from the ground."

"And what about this?" I said, touching the top of my head.

Mike and Pete mimicked the movement. Pete had a similar streak in his hair, running diagonally from left to right, while Mike's ran diagonally from right to left.

Both just shrugged.

"Are you guys scared?" I asked.

They looked at each other before Mike said, "A little."

"Me, too," Pete said.

"I'm glad I'm not the only one," I responded. "What are we going to do?"

"I don't know, but whatever it is, we need to stick together."

Mike held his hand out, palm down, and Pete and I did the same, meeting in the middle like a three-spoke wheel.

# CHAPTER 4
# RELEASED

We spent a few more days in the hospital. Various doctors performed a battery of tests: CT scans of our heads; cervical spine X-rays; urine drug screens; finger stick glucose; CBC blood chemistries; full physical exams; EKGs; and arterial blood gas tests, to name a few. Everything came up normal. The doctors were as in the dark as we were.

When we weren't being poked and prodded, we were being questioned. The local police visited on three occasions. They questioned us separately and together. I felt like a suspect in an old film noir police procedural. The only thing missing was someone handcuffing me to a table and shining a bright light in my eyes. None of us had any useful information, and our stories were the same. They either believed us or were convinced we had made up the whole thing. We could never really be sure.

Once the medical professionals decided there was nothing physically wrong and they could do nothing for us, they discharged us. The police had decided that either we were telling the truth, or there was not enough evidence of wrongdoing to charge us with any crime.

We were free to go.

●●●

It was too depressing to hang around the house, but I also didn't want to go out without Pete and Mike. Both their parents thought it best if they didn't go out or communicate, so I stayed in my room and read. Science fiction, mostly. Heinlein and Asimov were my favorites. It was a great way to escape without going anywhere.

My uncle Jim came by to check on me, although I suspected he was really monitoring my mother. Since we vanished, her drinking had worsened—far beyond what I thought possible. From my bedroom, I could hear him pleading with her to get help, but she refused to listen.

After three days of eating Kraft macaroni and cheese with chocolate milk, I knew I needed to get out of the house, with or without the guys. As I was getting ready to leave, the telephone rang. Knowing my mother wouldn't be able to answer it, I ran down the stairs two at a time and yanked the receiver from its cradle.

"Hello."

"Jack." It was Pete.

"Man, am I ever happy to hear your voice. How you doing?"

"Going stir crazy. I've been driving my mother nuts, so she finally said I could go out. I just talked to Mike. He's been pardoned, too. Let's go."

I never thought I could be made so happy by such simple words.

"On my way."

●●●

Of course, we went to The Park. It didn't occur to me not to. Heading to The Park was a natural thing to do, like breathing. When we got there, it seemed we were the only ones that still thought of it as natural. It felt deserted. Abandoned. And beneath it all, something felt unmistakably wrong.

We were at one of the benches near the drinking fountain, at a fork in the path. Older kids usually reserved this spot, and being able to sit there seemed like an opportunity, so we took it. I sat on top of the bench back, Pete on the bench, and Mike stood with his foot on the bench's seat, making it easy to see one another.

"Where is everybody?" I asked.

"My mom didn't want me coming here," Pete admitted. "I guess everybody else felt the same way."

"Yeah," said Mike. "My dad told me everybody was freaking out about us disappearing. Since it happened here, well, I guess they feel The Park had something to do with it."

"That's crazy, isn't it?" I said.

Neither of them responded as they nervously shifted their positions.

"Isn't it?" I reiterated. "I mean, come on. What could this

place have to do with it?"

"I guess people think that, whatever happened, it had to have involved somebody, and that somebody must have been here," Mike finally said.

"If you think about it," Pete offered, "it makes sense." When neither of us replied, he continued. "It's not like we disappeared on our own. Right?"

Mike was surveying our surroundings as he said, "Right."

I was astonished and totally clueless. "Why didn't you guys say something?"

They looked at each other, searching for an answer, before Pete said, "I don't know. I guess we didn't know where else to go."

"Are you creeped out at being here?" I asked.

Mike nodded as Pete said, "A little, yeah."

I jumped off my perch and grabbed my bike, startling the others. "What are you waiting for? Let's go."

They scurried to their bikes, and as they mounted, I said, "Just do me one favor. Let's ride over to the grass where they found us."

They peered at me as if I were the Creature from the Black Lagoon. It wasn't hard to surmise what they were thinking. I don't know if it was because of how well I knew them, but I was certain I could feel their anxiety. Physically feel it. I shook it off as being a figment of my imagination.

"I just want to satisfy my curiosity. I don't believe this place had anything to do with what happened, and we'll definitely be able to see if anybody is there before we get too close." Their skepticism did not abate. "Please."

Without another word, they climbed onto their bikes, and we shot off toward the line where the blacktop met the open field. Not even Merlin could have conjured the magic of that last ride.

●●●

We approached the target location carefully and methodically. Again, we rode three abreast, ensuring that none of us would arrive before the others. I focused on the area I thought might be where they had found us and couldn't see anything out of the ordinary. Nobody lurking in the open and nowhere to hide. As we approached, I glanced at my friends. They, too, focused on the same area. We got slowly closer, and all seemed well to me. Suddenly, I felt confusion emanating from them both, but different types of confusion. From Mike, it was mixed with fear. From Pete, something harder to pinpoint. I looked over at him to find he had stopped pedaling and was standing still, his bike cradled between his legs and his hands covering his ears. Mike and I both stopped and went to him.

"What's wrong?" I asked.

"Make it stop," he pleaded.

"Make what stop?" asked Mike.

"The noise."

Neither Mike nor I heard anything, but now there was no mistaking the fear coming from both Pete and Mike. Mike looked at me for an answer.

"Come on. Let's ride away from here," I urged. When Pete didn't move, I gave him a friendly nudge. "Hey. Let's go."

That did it. As fast as we could, we turned and rode back in the direction from which we had come.

●●●

We rode to Little Louies, another local hot dog joint. This was Chicago, and our neighborhood had three such places within a block of one another. We chose Louies because it actually had a storefront with booths, unlike the other two. We tried to ignore the stares coming our way as we walked to the back booth, hoping for some privacy. The murmurings that followed us made ignoring everyone else an impossible task.

A server brought us glasses of water and asked for our order. We each ordered Cokes and shared a plate of fries. A quiet encompassed our table as if a cone of silence had covered it. After our server delivered our order, we picked at the food.

"So," Mike said, gazing at me, "your curiosity satisfied?"

An ironic laugh escaped before I could stop it. "Not really," I answered.

"Why is that?" Pete asked as he chewed.

"Because," I said, "what the hell was that!?!" It seemed the other patrons were trying to listen to our conversation, so I lowered my voice in a futile attempt at privacy. "I didn't see or hear anything. But you, Pete, definitely heard something." Turning my attention to Mike, I continued, "And you, Mike, were definitely afraid of something. What am I missing?"

"I wasn't afraid," Mike protested.

I stared at him until his gaze became centered on the table.

"Don't ask me how," I said, "but I could feel the fear. From both of you."

"What do you mean?" asked Pete.

"Just that. It was weird, but I could tell what you were feeling. Almost physically feel it." They stared at me blankly. "The first time I felt it, at the bench today, I thought I was imagining it. But this last time, it was definitely not my imagination."

I felt the agitation rising, so I took a long sip of Coke through the straw, hoping it would settle me down.

"What happened to us?" I asked.

Nobody had an answer.

"Pete, tell us what you heard."

He didn't answer immediately, and we let him take his time. When he had gathered his composure enough to speak, but not to look at us, he said, "I'm not sure I can describe it. At first, it was a voice." He looked up at us. "A screaming voice. Then it was more than one voice, and then just a bunch of voices, all screaming." With an imploring look, he said, "I think they were in pain. It was awful." We didn't know what to say, so we said nothing. The silence pressed down on us, heavy and unbearable.

"Mike, what about you?" I asked.

"What about me?"

"Listen, I know you were afraid. It's nothing to be ashamed of. We're all freaked out. But what was it for you?"

I knew I shouldn't push it, but I had to know. Our eyes locked, and we silently dared each other to be the first to look away. He was the first to blink, metaphorically speaking. "I could feel the place. The evil of the place. It was like it was warning me away. Or daring me to keep going. I couldn't tell which."

Unheard of in our brief lives, almost a full plate of fries remained, getting cold enough so that the grease coagulated. To anybody able to read the situation, it clearly indicated the level of intensity at our table.

"Maybe everybody staying away from The Park wasn't such a bad idea," I ventured.

"Maybe," my companions agreed.

I felt as if someone had ripped my one safe space from the universe, leaving me alone and vulnerable.

# CHAPTER 5
# TRYING TO FIGURE IT OUT

Pete and Mike had been instructed to stay home, so I was on my own. Without having The Park as a place to go, and not wanting to stay home and watch my mother drink herself to death, I found myself at the Northtown branch of the Chicago Public Library. It was not a large branch, but was the closest to my house. Even then, I was not allowed to ride that far alone. I needed something to do and figured nobody would really give me a hard time about it. I wasn't wrong.

The things we had each experienced at The Park had my mind racing. Why were they happening? Where were we for three days? What had happened during that time? Had it happened to others? My plan was to do some research. The library had a reference section, a couple of microfilm readers, and lots of old newspapers to read on them.

●●●

At ten-years-old I had little experience with this type of research, so I asked the reference librarian for help. I thought a logical place to begin would be with the disappearance of other kids. Her reaction surprised me.

"Isn't that a little morbid for someone of your age, young man?"

I wasn't sure what "morbid" meant, but took a chance and

said, "No, ma'am. I don't think so. It could be really important." When she made no move to help, I said, "Please."

She stared at me for a moment, her gaze finally landing on the top of my head. I could see understanding dawn. "You're one of the boys that went missing recently, aren't you?"

I cast my eyes to the floor and said, "Yes, ma'am."

That seemed to make all the difference.

"Wait here and I'll bring you some microfilm of newspaper articles."

I followed her instructions and waited. And waited. She must have decided my unexplained disappearance warranted the effort, because fifteen minutes later she returned with a stack of microfilm and a scrap of paper covered in notes.

"Here you go, young man. I made some notes as to where you might find relevant information."

I thanked her as I accepted her offering and turned to make my way to the microfilm reader.

"Would you like me to show you how to use that?"

I turned to her and smiled. "Yes, please. That would be great."

She left her domain and walked with me to a waiting machine. I listened carefully as she instructed me on its use. When I completed the lesson, I said, "Thank you, ma'am," and felt a bewildering emotion from her.

It was that day I learned what a powerful force pity could be.

●●●

I started with the list the librarian had provided. She had gone back twenty years for city-wide statistics. I didn't know what to expect, but it wasn't forty-nine cases in 1950, alone. That's almost one a week! The numbers fluctuated over the years, some years having more and some less. Still, the sheer volume of missing persons staggered me.

Having exhausted the list for the 1950s, I moved on to the 1960s, which had almost identical statistics. The big news of the 60s involved Richard Speck, a career criminal and mass murderer. In July 1966, he bound, attacked, raped, and murdered eight nursing students. The city never fully recovered. One change was that people paid more attention when children went missing, not that they could do anything about it. In 1970, parents were still pretty open to letting their kids roam the neighborhood, unsupervised.

Then I got to 1968. I should have been ready for it—but wasn't.

*Body of Ten-Year-Old Boy Found on North Side*

The headline hit me like the right hand of Muhammad Ali. I had to grab the table to stop from hitting the floor as I went down for the count.

When I had recovered enough to think, I needed to decide

whether to read the story or move to the next. The decision was made without my overt consent, as I looked at the screen and couldn't tear my eyes from the words:

*The body of Ralph Steven Winterhaven, age 10, was discovered yesterday along the banks of the north branch of the Chicago River. Two youths, whose parents asked that their identities not be revealed, were scavenging along the banks of the waterway when they came upon the remains of young Winterhaven. Ralph was last seen by his mother three days prior when he said he was going for a bicycle ride. His whereabouts during that ride remain unknown. An extensive search of the area around the north side neighborhood where Ralph Winterhaven lived was conducted by both neighbors and the police. His body was discovered approximately five miles from his home. No further information has been released by the police. If you have any information regarding this matter, please contact the Chicago Police Department at 555-5970.*

I took a moment to let the words fully worm their way into my mind. When they had, a couple of things stood out: first, that Ralph was discovered five miles from home, and second, that he had been gone three days before he had been discovered. I don't know if it was because I was only eight years old when he disappeared, but I never really understood how far away from home someone found him. The three days hadn't meant anything before, but now the time period held more import, as I too had been missing for three days. Could there be a connection, or was it merely a coincidence?

Was he actually gone three days, or had he been dumped before that and only found after three days? If the latter, then it was harder to connect to my case. Anyway, it didn't seem that there was a way to know for certain.

I was emotionally drained and physically exhausted. Research, I discovered, was incredibly tiring. I gathered the microfilm reels, turned the machine off, and returned the materials to the librarian.

"Thank you, young man. Did you find what you were looking for?"

"Well, ma'am, I'm not really sure what I was looking for, but it sure was interesting."

She gave me a quizzical look as I headed out the door.

●●●

"Hey, Mom. Can I ask you a question?"

She looked away from the television, which was an encouraging development.

"Sure, honey. What is it?"

"Did anybody ever find Ralphie's bicycle?"

I thought I'd start with what should have been a simple question. As soon as I asked it, I could see her discomfort grow, evidenced by the fact she immediately reached for the ever-present glass of vodka.

She took a long gulp before saying, "Not that I know of.

Why?"

"I was just wondering, that's all." I took a gulp of air to calm my nerves before asking the next question. It didn't work. "Mom, do you know if they found Ralphie the same day he was left at the river, or if he'd been there for a while before they found him?"

I was hoping for a calm, measured answer. Instead, I watched as she clenched her jaw; the muscles working as if chewing a tough piece of meat. Her eyebrows furrowed, and her face turned a color of crimson I'd only seen in movie scenes of wildfires. She raised her glass as if preparing to throw it at me when she seemed to realize how precious its contents were and, instead, took a quick gulp of liquid.

Her voice reached a high pitch, and the volume was as loud as I'd ever heard her as she screamed, "Why would you ask me that!?! Why do you want to torture me!?! Get out! Go on, just get out!"

Mortified, I slunk out of the room as the tears poured down her face. I bolted upstairs, slammed my door, and collapsed onto the bed, burying my face in the pillow, struggling to breathe.

●●●

An hour later, I ventured downstairs and found her passed out on the couch, the television still on. I tried to stay quiet, but the floor creaked—and she jolted awake.

"Hi, honey. Are you hungry?"

I didn't know what to expect, but not that.

"Yes, I am," I answered.

"OK. Can you make something?"

I didn't think she was in any condition to cook, so said, "Yeah, sure." I turned to go into the kitchen, but stopped and went back into the living room. "Mom, are you OK?"

"Yes, dear. Why wouldn't I be?"

"No reason. Just checking."

"Well, thank you, dear."

With her attention back on the television, I made my way to the kitchen, totally mystified. How is it possible that she has no memory of our last encounter? Before making my peanut butter and jelly sandwich, I detoured to the yellow rotary dial wall phone hanging on a kitchen wall. Once I heard the dial tone, I called my uncle Jim.

"Hello."

"Hi, Uncle Jim. It's Jack."

"Hey, Jack. Is everything all right?"

I told him about my earlier conversation with my mom and her total lack of recall.

"Is that normal?"

"Jack, for somebody who drinks as much as your mom, it's not unheard of for them to be forgetful."

"I had no idea. Is she going to be OK?"

"I wish I could tell you, but unless she stops drinking, I'm afraid she's not going to be OK."

Silence enveloped us as I drank that information in.

"Jack?"

"Sorry, Uncle Jim."

"Jack, if you ever need me to come over, just call. I'll do what I can."

"Thank you. I appreciate it."

When neither of us said anything else, he said, "Is there anything else you want from me?"

I was about to respond in the negative, but said, "Yes. Can you answer the question I asked mom? Do you know if Ralph had been out there for a while before they found him, or if he was left there that same day?"

"Based on the amount of decomposition, the police thought he had been left there not too much before he was found. Why are you asking?"

"Well," I said, "with my disappearance, I just had some questions. Thank you for being honest with me."

"I understand, Jack. Let me know if you have any other questions."

"Will do. Thanks."

And just like that, unbeknownst to me, a seed was planted in my mind.

# CHAPTER 6
# SO WHAT NOW?

"So, what do you think?" I asked.

Since The Park was off-limits, the three of us had convened in Pete's basement, most of which was taken up by the full-size billiard table. Instead of playing pool, I absentmindedly rolled the balls back and forth across the table while recounting my day at the library and my conversation with my uncle.

"About what?" Mike asked.

"About all the missing kids and especially Ralphie," I said, unable to hide the exasperation in my voice as I flung a ball just a little too hard.

"I don't know," Pete chimed in. "So, a lot of kids go missing. Most are either found dead or never turn up. What does any of that have to do with us?"

"And Ralphie's having been gone for three days is only a coincidence, Jack," added Mike. "What difference does it make if the kids are missing for one, two, three, or a hundred days?"

Deflated, I shoved a ball into a pocket and said, "I don't know. I was just looking for answers. A connection to something else, maybe." When neither of them responded, I said, "Aren't either of you curious about what happened?"

"Sure, I'm curious," Pete said. "I just don't have any idea about how to get any answers."

When I looked at Mike, he shrugged and remained silent.

"What about what happened the last time we were at The Park?" I said. "Mike, have you felt that evil again?"

"No." Short and to the point.

"Pete, what about you? Hear any voices?"

"I haven't been out of the house much since then, but no, I haven't."

Mike asked, "What about you, Jack? Have you felt any feelings from anybody else since then?"

The pause in my response told them everything they needed to know.

"No way!" said Pete. "Tell us."

I told them about my conversation with the librarian. How I could sense her pity, and how I managed to turn that to my advantage.

"Well, at least one of us got something useful," Mike muttered.

I could feel what had to be jealousy radiating from him, as he said it. I thought it best not to comment and instead launched a ball down the table.

After an interminable silence, I said, "So, what now?"

We just stared at each other. No one had an answer, something that never happened. It was then I knew something vital had shifted within each of us.

"How 'bout if we just try to enjoy what's left of the summer?" Pete suggested.

"How?" asked Mike.

"Let's just pretend everything's normal," Pete said. "We've only got a couple of weeks left before school. Let's go to the beach. Or some other parks."

"Okay, let's do that," I agreed. "Mike?"

"Let's give it a shot."

And that's what we did.

# CHAPTER 7
# BACK IN SCHOOL

Summer was over, and we were back in school. The fifth grade. Unlike other places, Chicago didn't have junior high schools. Elementary school consisted of kindergarten through eighth grade, meaning we were at the mercy of the older kids. Depending on your social status, it could be a particularly trying time to be a kid.

My social status had usually been pretty middle-of-the-road, which meant I could generally avoid getting picked on. It didn't take long for me to learn of a change to the status quo. Walking to my locker, I heard someone say, "Hey, it's skunk boy." I didn't bother looking for the speaker but knew he was referring to the white streak in my hair. Ignoring him seemed to be the best solution, as I wasn't much of a fighter. Pete had the same reaction as me when someone said something about his diagonal streak. Mike, however, wasn't putting up with it. During the first week of school, he'd punched a seventh grader in the mouth and was sent to the principal's office. The principal, Dr. Elkin, a short, balding man in his fifties, knew of Mike's summer ordeal and took pity on him, letting him go with a warning and punishing his tormentor with extra homework. That helped put a stop to the overt bullying, but did little to stop the more subtle kind we faced whenever the chance presented itself.

There were four different fifth-grade classrooms and Mike,

Pete, and I were each in different ones, which meant we couldn't count on each other for support during most of the school day. Much of the time that was okay, with some of our classmates being curious as to what had happened to us, but not obnoxious about it. Still, even among the other students, I felt isolated and alone much of the time.

●●●

Recess and physical education were, weather permitting, held outside. First through third grades had recess at 10:00 a.m., fourth through sixth grades at 10:45 a.m., and seventh and eighth grades at 1:00 p.m. The staggered times worked in our favor, as far as bullying was concerned.

We spent recess in the playground and, together with our classmates, were able to just have fun. Pete, Mike, and I refrained from talking about anything having to do with the disappearance during school hours because we could never be certain others wouldn't hear.

Physical education, a/k/a gym, was a different story. They held gym class either on the blacktop behind the school or on the adjacent grass field. All four classrooms had gym together if the weather was warm enough, so I could be with both Pete and Mike when that happened.

One of the outdoor activities was a jog around the field. The three of us were able to run together most of the time. The gym teacher, Mr. Korak, led us around the perimeter of the field and back towards the school, which necessitated our passing through the area where we had been found. Nobody except us was aware of the fact, so they didn't give it a moment's thought. As soon as we made the turn for the home stretch, I could feel both Pete and Mike tense up.

As quietly as possible, I said. "Keep it together."

They both looked at me, understanding that I could feel their trepidation. The closer we got to the target area, the more I could feel their fear. For Pete, it was the fear of hearing voices. For Mike, it was the fear of the evil which emanated from the place.

"Let's sprint," I called out, taking off ahead. A quick glance over my shoulder told me they were both right behind me. As we sped past the scene of the crime, I could feel their fear dissipate. When we got to the building, we stopped, bent over with hands on our knees, and breathed hard.

"Good idea," Mike sputtered.

"Yeah, that really helped," Pete said between gasps for air.

I just nodded, too out of breath to speak. When I could finally say something, I asked, "Did either of you feel anything?"

They each looked around before whispering.

"I started to hear voices."

"And I could feel the place. Running past helped."

Before any of us could say another word, Mr. Korak walked up, came to a stop, and said, "Good job, boys."

We croaked out, "Thanks," as he headed back inside.

We met after school and walked home together, following the reverse of our pickup route. When we arrived at Mike's house, we stopped and gathered on his front steps.

"Something weird is definitely going on at The Park," I opened.

"That's for sure," Pete said. "What the hell is it about that place?"

We waited for Mike to say something. When he did, it wasn't anything we expected.

"I haven't been totally honest with you guys," he said, his eyes downcast.

We remained silent until he looked up at us.

"I went somewhere with my dad the other day. We drove in his car."

We knew there had to be more. When he offered nothing further, Pete said, "And?"

"And there were a few places we passed where I had the same feeling. The feeling of evil. Calling to me."

"Like you could hear it call your name?" asked Pete.

Mike shook his head as he said, "No. It wasn't anything I could actually hear. It was a feeling." His eyes were pleading. "It scared me."

"Where were you when it happened?" I asked.

"I don't know. I wasn't really paying attention. Just staring out the window into space."

I pressed on. "What kind of places were they? Were they open spaces, like The Park, or were they buildings, or something else?"

He thought before answering. "Now that you mention it, I think they were open spaces. At least a couple of times. I know I looked up and, yeah, they were definitely open spaces."

"Wow," Pete said.

"Yeah," I said. "That's big. Like, it's not just The Park or where we were found." To Pete, I said, "How about you? Have you heard any voices anyplace else?"

He shook his head and said, "No, but I really haven't left the neighborhood."

"The next time your mom has to drive someplace, ask if you could go with her. You know, to help," I suggested.

I could feel his reluctance before he said, "OK. I will."

"Great!" Reaching for my backpack, I said, "I have to get home."

"Me too," Pete said, as he grabbed his backpack and we prepared to continue our journey.

"There's something else," Mike interjected, stopping Pete

and me in our tracks. When he had our attention, Mike continued. "One time I felt something, but it wasn't a place."

"What do you mean?" I asked.

"I had that feeling. You know, like I could feel the evil. So I looked out the window. I expected to see a park or something like that. Instead, I saw a man. He was wearing a suit and carrying a briefcase, just like a hundred of the other guys walking around. But as soon as I looked up, he stopped. Suddenly, like he'd hit an invisible wall. He stopped, turned, and locked eyes with me. I don't think either of us blinked. We kept staring at each other as he stood there and we drove away."

Well, that was definitely something else.

# CHAPTER 8
# A CONVERSATION WITH SHERLOCK

When I got home, the house was empty. I found a note on the kitchen table:

*Hi, Jack. I took your mom to the grocery store. We won't be too long. Jim*

Knowing that my mother hadn't actually cooked a meal in a very long time, I thought, "I hope there's stuff that's easy for me to make." I crumbled the note and threw it in the trash before removing a cold bottle of Kayo from the fridge, opening it, and bounding up the stairs to my room.

●●●

I kicked my shoes off, sat on the bed, and brought my feet up. I had to concentrate on not chugging the Kayo because I wanted it to last as long as possible. Slow, measured sips. It was torture.

Having the house to myself allowed me to converse openly with my room without worrying about being overheard.

"So, Mike can feel evil from a person. Interesting."

When nobody was available to converse with, pretending to have a conversation with someone helped me process information. An adult with great powers of deduction.

Someone like Sherlock Holmes.

"Yes, it is," responded Sherlock. "But what do you think it means?"

"Well, obviously, it means he can feel evil from a person."

"Don't, young man, be a smartass," Sherlock scolded.

"OK, OK."

I thought for what felt like a long time. "It means that whatever abilities we received during our disappearance are not just tied to that one place. He felt evil in other places, in addition to that guy. I think it means Pete is going to hear voices at other places, too."

"Agreed," said Sherlock. "It really shouldn't come as too much of a surprise to you."

"Why?"

"Think about it, Jack. Where were you when you realized you could feel someone's emotions? Someone other than Pete or Mike."

As instructed, I thought about it. "The library."

"Exactly. The library. Neither Pete nor Mike were anywhere near, and you were far from The Park. If you could use that new ability elsewhere, it only makes sense that they could do so too, don't you think?"

"Now that you mention it, Sherlock, I do think."

"So," Sherlock said, "now that you know your abilities are real and portable, what do you think you need to do?"

I was out of answers—and out of patience for his mind games.

"You're a smart guy. You tell me."

"OK, if I must," he replied. "Although I am disappointed you didn't come up with the answer on your own."

"Sorry to disappoint, but, please, I'm tired. Just tell me."

"It seems to me that, with your having these abilities and knowing you could use them anywhere, you'd want to know how to control them. Use them by choice, not when they are imposed upon you," Sherlock said.

Impressed, I said, "You really are a smart guy, Sherlock. If we could control the abilities, it would be very helpful. Thank you."

He nodded his appreciation and disappeared just as I finished my drink and closed my eyes.

●●●

I woke to the sound of the front door opening, jumped out of bed, and went downstairs. I noticed Uncle Jim walking toward the kitchen with groceries in hand, but there was no sign of my mother. When I finally reached the bottom of the stairs, I saw her lounging in her usual spot on the couch.

"Hey, Mom. How are you?"

"Hi, honey. I'm good. Come here and give your mother a kiss."

I thought she looked pale, thin, and fragile, but didn't say so. Instead, I gave her a kiss on the cheek just as Jim came into the room.

"Hi, Uncle Jim. How was grocery shopping?"

"It was fine. I left the bag on the counter because I'm not sure where everything goes."

I knew they were both lying to me. I felt it. Something wasn't as they wanted me to believe.

"Where did you go besides the grocery store?" I asked.

With expressions that blank, they might as well have been poker champs. If I couldn't feel their emotions, I'd never have known they were trying to keep something from me. Except for the quick glance they gave each other, there was no physical tell.

"Nowhere, dear. Just shopping."

"Well, that's not technically true, Karla, is it?

I could feel his confidence growing and my mom getting worried as if she were concerned about what he was going to say next.

"Well, no, Jim. It isn't."

She was playing along, but still worried.

"We stopped for a cup of coffee and a piece of pie. We should have brought a piece back for you. I'm sorry I didn't think of it earlier."

He was confident he'd covered his tracks, but I knew better. Rather than push it, I just nodded and went to unpack the groceries.

What had they been up to? I didn't know, but I had a feeling this new ability was going to come in handy.

# CHAPTER 9
# PRACTICE

"How are we supposed to do that?" Pete said, his voice rising. "It's not like we can find a teacher or anything."

Back on the steps of Mike's house, I filled them in on what Sherlock and I had figured out—minus the part about Sherlock. There were just some things I felt weird about sharing, and my penchant for talking to absent fictional characters fit squarely in that category.

"I didn't say I knew how to do it. Only that it would be a good idea." I didn't want to come across as being defensive, but couldn't help it.

Mike had been listening and broke his silence by saying, "How do you teach yourself anything?" Answering his own question, he continued, "Like my dad taught me, you practice and learn by trial and error."

"Wait," said Pete. "By trial and error, do you mean we have to put ourselves in a place where you feel the fear and I hear voices? On purpose?"

"I don't see any other way," Mike answered.

"Well, that doesn't sound like a great idea. I'm more in the let's avoid those places at all costs camp," Pete said.

"Then how would you get control over hearing the voices?

You're not always going to be able to avoid those places. Wouldn't you rather be prepared, knowing what to do?"

Pete shuffled his feet as he said, "Yeah. I guess so. The thought of doing it just creeps me out."

"Let's be sure we try it out together. Jack, you'll come, too, won't you?"

"Definitely," I said.

"Since Jack isn't really affected in the same way, he can pull us out of it. Just like at gym."

I could feel Pete letting go of his wariness as he said, "That makes sense." He turned his attention to me and said, "What about you, Jack? How are you going to get control?"

"I guess the same as you guys," I said. "It doesn't seem I need to be in any particular place. Just around people. So, I can work on shutting it off when I want to. I think."

"Why do I have a bad feeling about this?" asked Pete.

●●●

We gathered on the following weekend, one of the last halfway decent days of the year. It was November, a little over three months after our disappearance. No more shorts and tee-shirts, that was for sure. Jeans, sweatshirts, and jackets. At least there was no snow, so we could still ride our bikes.

The plan was to revisit the site of our discovery at The Park.

Since it was the only place we knew for certain had affected us, with "us" being primarily Pete and Mike, we figured it to be the logical starting point.

Our ride over was more somber than in the past. The joy had been lost and the hole in my soul widened. One of the best parts of my youth had been stolen. The one safe space I could always count on had been stripped from me, and I had no idea how to get it back.

As we approached the target area, I could feel my friends' growing nervousness. Since I didn't share the same type of effects from whatever our ordeal had been, I wasn't as nervous, but, truth be told, I was still worried. Not so much for myself, but still.

Without communicating in any conscious way, we slowed our roll as we got closer. Under the circumstances, caution was not a bad thing. We crept forward, each step slower than the last, until we arrived at what seemed to be the spot. I could feel the uncertainty in my companions, but unlike before, it carried a strange undercurrent of relief.

"What is it?" I asked.

They didn't answer immediately. Instead, they looked at each other and closed their eyes in concentration. After a minute, both opened their eyes and looked at me.

"I can barely feel any evil. Maybe a hint. A slight trace at most."

Surprised, I said, "Pete?"

"The same. I can sort of hear the voices, but they aren't bombarding me. Like Mike said, a hint of the voices being there."

I looked at our surroundings, trying to see if anything had changed. Nothing I could see.

"Interesting," was all I could manage.

●●●

We rode to the playground to confer. Enough time had passed that people no longer felt The Park to be an obvious threat, so the older kids had reclaimed the bench. It was too bad because it made me feel just a little older. More confident. The Park hierarchy pushed us back to our usual place in the playground.

There were a couple of parents and their young kids at the monkey bars, so we scooted under the turtles for some privacy.

"So," I began, "what do you think?"

"I think maybe it's a good thing I can't hear voices anymore," Pete said.

I could feel his relief.

"Do you think that's what it is?" asked Mike.

"What else could it be?"

Mike snuck a peek in my direction before answering. "I don't know. I could still feel evil. It just wasn't...as threatening. Like it was far away."

"I thought you said you could hear voices. Just that they were faint," I said.

Reluctantly, Pete said, "Yeah, I could. But maybe it's because the 'ability', if that's what you want to call it, is fading. Just going away."

"Maybe." I could feel the confidence in his position wavering. "But you don't really think so, do you?"

"Fuck you, Jack! Stop trying to read my mind!"

Before I could respond, he scampered out from under the turtle and stomped off toward the drinking fountain.

"I think you might have hit a nerve there, Jack."

"I might have," I said, as I moved to follow Pete.

Mike's hand shot out, halting me in my tracks.

"Let him walk it off. He'll be back."

It was good advice, and I took it. While we waited, Mike said, "You haven't chimed in. What do you think?"

"I think I agree with you. If your abilities were gone, you wouldn't be able to pick anything up. Maybe it's like a radio signal. You know, like when we try listening to a baseball game from New York, or somewhere like that. The farther away it is, the harder it is to pick up."

"And maybe whatever it is, or was, moved away."

"Maybe."

Just as Mike had predicted, Pete came back to the protection of the turtle.

"Sorry. I didn't mean to swear at you like that."

I smiled and said, "That's OK, Pete. I bet it felt good, though."

He laughed and said, "It did."

We told him about our radio signal theory and he took it much better than I expected. Before leaving the safety of the turtle, we decided that the only way to test our theory was to find another site that might yield some results, like one of the places Mike had passed while in the car with his dad. Mike agreed to talk to his father and attempt to figure out where that might be.

If Pete was right, it might be the end of our ordeal. If our radio signal theory was right, it might mean we had a chance to figure out what happened. It would be nice if both could be true.

# CHAPTER 10
# LITTLE LIES

Mike had successfully discovered from his father where a couple of those other parks were located. He had to be less than open and honest about it, but, through feigned interest in their trip, discerned the route they had taken. It was a little too far to take our bikes, but the Chicago Transit Authority busses went where we needed them to go. For the princely sum of fifty-five cents, which included a dime for a transfer, we could make the round trip, returning before anybody knew we were gone.

●●●

The first park was Mather, the location of Mather High School. Located at California and Peterson Avenues, it was a straight shot up California Avenue on the number 94 bus. We boarded at Touhy Avenue and found seats. Our nervous energy was almost palpable. Words were scarce, yet the restless bouncing of our legs felt like enough to run a nuclear submarine.

Twenty minutes later, we got off the bus. Standing on the corner of California and Peterson Avenues, we looked around, nervously getting our bearings.

"This way," Mike directed. We followed as he crossed the street to the park proper. I could feel the tension rising in my cohorts.

"You guys OK?" I asked.

"We'll find out," Pete answered. Mike just nodded and kept walking.

We walked the perimeter and, when neither of them felt anything, crisscrossed the park using a grid pattern of about ten feet. When we reached the middle of the park, we stopped. I could feel their concentration, but both remained relatively calm.

"I can feel a little of the fear, but it's even fainter than at The Park. What about you, Pete?"

"Maybe a whisper, but not much else."

"Hmm. OK, let's go over to the next place. It's right down the street."

As Mike strode off, fully expecting us to follow, which we did, Pete said, "I think I'm losing any ability to hear the voices. They were so faint I'm not even sure I heard anything. It could just be background noise. You know, the cars, their tires, people talking."

I could tell he was trying just as hard to convince himself as he was trying to convince us. Both Mike and I remained silent as we drudged along. We walked west on Peterson Avenue for about six blocks until we came to Kedzie Avenue, where Hollywood Park was located. We had no idea why it was called that, especially since it had nothing to do with Hollywood or movies. Another one of those strange mysteries of youth.

Similar to Rogers Park, Hollywood Park had a playground, basketball courts, and baseball diamonds. Unlike either Rogers or Mather, it did not have a school. Instead of walking around this park, as we had at Mather, Mike strode purposefully to the center of the grass field. I could sense the self-assurance in the way he moved. Pete and I kept a short distance behind, and seeing Pete walk just as steadily told me he wasn't being haunted by any whispers today. Then Mike came to an abrupt stop. When we caught up to him, Pete stood right next to him and I could feel his confidence fade and his fear and anger rise. He must be hearing something. Mike was working hard at keeping his fear in control, and for the most part, it was working. When Mike felt he was under control, he ventured forward, gently taking Pete's arm and forcing him to go along. I followed closely behind, concentrating on their emotions. Mike was forcing his fear into the back of his mind, moving forward ever slowly. Pete was trying. I could feel his effort, but his emotions were getting the better of him. When Mike stopped once again, Pete stood next to him while I hung back a few steps.

"What do you hear, Pete?" Mike said.

"I hear voices, dammit. Louder than they were at either The Park or Mather, but not like that first time. What do you feel?"

Mike was nodding his head as if confirming something to himself, as he said, "Evil. I can feel evil. But, like you said, stronger than the last time at The Park and at Mather, but nowhere near as strong as the first time. Not threatening."

Without moving forward, I said, "Pete, can you try to block the voices out?"

He didn't answer, but I could feel his concentration. Followed shortly thereafter by frustration. "Not really. They just won't go away, even though they're not all that loud."

"Let's move back and then walk here again while you try to stop hearing them at all," Mike suggested.

They did so while I waited. I worked on reaching out to feel their emotions and found, if I concentrated enough, I could feel them from farther and farther. The problem was I could also feel other people who were at the park. I'd need to work on narrowing my focus.

As they walked back to my position, it became easier for me to focus on just the two of them. Pete was really working on blocking out the voices, but I could tell he wasn't successful, even before they reached me and stopped.

"I just can't do it. No matter how hard I try, they won't go away," he said, trying to hold back tears.

"Don't worry about it," I encouraged. "This is the first try. I've been trying to focus on just the two of you and haven't been able to block out everybody else, especially when you were far away."

"And I still can't get rid of my fear," Mike said.

I think our confessions helped to calm Pete. He said, "OK,

thanks. Let's try it again."

That he wanted to try was an encouraging sign. We repeated the exercise, with me maintaining my position. I had a little more success in focusing on them than the last time. As they walked back towards me, I could feel Mike purge himself of fear while Pete struggled to block the voices out.

"So?" asked Mike.

Pete shook his head as he said, "The same."

"Yeah, me too," said Mike, sending a furtive glance in my direction.

"Yep," I said. "No change," returning Mike's glance.

"Let's try it a couple of times more before we go home."

Pete checked his watch and agreed. We repeated the exercise twice more. Each time, Mike and I had improved results. Pete made no progress.

Mike reached out and touched Pete's arm. "Yeah, we all need to practice more," he said. "Maybe we can come back again."

"Yeah," I agreed. "What is it the adults always say? Practice makes perfect."

I felt some of the tension ease out of Pete.

Oh, the lies one tells one's friends when trying to do the right thing.

# CHAPTER 11
# GLAD WE COULD HELP

Over the following weeks, we took every opportunity we could to revisit both Mather and Hollywood parks. Even though fall had descended with a vengeance, we also began frequenting The Park on a more regular basis, as did everybody else in the neighborhood who could stand the cold. Any stigma attached to The Park had dissipated with time, and all seemed right with the world. At least our little corner of it. We were mostly left alone as long as we didn't overstep the boundaries of the reestablished unspoken hierarchy in The Park.

On our visits to Mather and Hollywood parks, we learned that, just as at The Park, time seemed to dispel the effects of whatever had caused the feeling of evil and the rise of the voices. As a result, our practices did not yield the results for which we had hoped, which was a disappointment for Mike and me. Pete, however, had continued to try to convince himself that the reason he and Mike couldn't detect any trace of evil or voices was because the ability to do so had vanished. He ignored the fact that my ability to detect emotions was as strong as ever. Instead, he argued that because my ability wasn't location-specific, it made sense that I still possessed it. Whatever. There was no argument strong enough to move him. There was only one thing that could do that, and it was beyond my control.

●●●

Mike and I dressed for the cold, wrapped like mummies who had escaped from the Field Museum. I wondered what we were going to do once the actual winter hit if this was how we reacted to fall. Maybe we were so cold because the warm weather was still fresh in our minds and the difference was so striking. Everybody else's clothing choices showed we weren't alone in our reactions.

We were walking across The Park on our way to The Hot Dog Shack. It was the weekend, and even though the temperature was only around forty-five degrees, the sun was shining, which was enough for Chicagoans to be outdoors. Consequently, there were quite a few people of all ages milling about. As we left the boundaries of The Park, Mike stopped abruptly in the middle of the street. I could feel his tension as his level of alertness rose.

"What is it?"

He was scanning our surroundings as he said, "Remember when I said I felt evil from that guy when I was with my dad?"

"Uh-huh," I replied, as I too scanned the area, not knowing what I was looking for.

"Same thing."

As we continued to inspect the surroundings, a car turned a corner down the block and came into view.

"There," Mike said, pointing.

As we watched, the car rolled slowly down the street, coming to a sudden stop. The passenger door flew open and a man wearing black clothing and a black ski mask emerged, ran to the sidewalk, and grabbed a kid, tucking him under his arm like Walter Payton running for the end zone. He ran back to the car, jumped in, and slammed the door shut. The car lurched forward and sped towards us as we stood motionless in the street, two deer staring at headlights. We could see the driver, also wearing a ski mask, and the passenger, struggling to get his cargo under control. The car swerved to avoid us at the last moment and I turned to follow its path. As I did so, I could see Mike silently mouthing something.

"Are you OK?" I asked Mike. He was unnaturally calm.

"JF 2742. JF 2742. JF 2742."

I repeated, "JF 2742."

We ran to the nearest house and banged on the door until someone pulled it open, obviously annoyed.

"What the hell do you think you're doing?" The speaker was a large, balding man with an overhanging gut. He held his can of Pabst Blue Ribbon in one hand while the other held the door open.

"Sorry, sir," I spat out. "We just witnessed a kidnapping and need you to call the police."

Beside me, Mike recited the license plate number like a Buddhist monk repeating a mantra.

I felt the man's irritation shift, melting into something more like disbelief.

I ramped up the pleading tone of my voice and spoke faster. "Please, mister. It was a light blue 1965 Chevy Impala, license plate JF 2742. We wouldn't make up something like this. We know how much trouble we'd get into."

That did it. His disbelief was now concern as he held the door open and said, "Come on. Let's call the cops together."

●●●

We waited in Mr. Zalesky's living room, known in Chicago as the "front room." Sitting on the plastic-covered sofa and drinking Coca-Cola from bottles, we waited for the police while Mr. Zalesky asked us about what had happened. We had just finished telling our story when there was a knock at the open door and our host rose to let the waiting police officers into his home.

When Mr. Zalesky pointed at Mike and me, the two uniformed officers strode to us, oozing authority.

"OK, boys. What's this all about?" asked Officer Podolsky, his name clearly stated on the nametag, which was part of his uniform.

Excitedly, we both began telling the tale, which caused Officer Podolsky to hold his hands up. "Slow down. One at a time." He pointed at me and said, "You. Go first."

I repeated the story, with Mike chipping in to make any necessary corrections and filling in the gaps. While Officer Podolsky sat in a wing chair facing us, his partner, Officer Hagerty, stood silently taking notes in an official-looking little black notebook.

"OK, boys. That's quite a story."

I could feel his skepticism. Turning to Mike, I said, "He doesn't believe us."

Defensively, Officer Podolsky said, "No, no. I want to believe you. It just boggles my mind to think that somebody would try to pull this off in broad daylight, is all."

I knew he was being less than truthful.

"Let me ask you something," the officer continued, directing his question at me, confident he was about to trip me up. "How can you be so certain the car was a 1965 Chevy Impala? How do you know it wasn't a 1964 or 1967?"

Like many boys my age, I looked forward to the release of the new car models, eager to see what changes had been made.

"Because," I said, not trying to hide my exasperation, "the 1964 body style was totally different from the 1965. And the taillights of the 1967 were different from the 1965 taillights. 1965 had three round lights on each side. 1967 had flat taillights." I glared at him in defiance.

He looked at his partner, who nodded and said, "The kid's right."

Rising from his seat, Officer Podolsky said, "OK boys. We'll look into this. Give my partner your names, phone numbers, and addresses in case we have any follow-up questions."

"That's it?" asked Mike.

"For now, yes. That's it."

As he walked to the door, his portable radio squawked. The officer stepped onto the front porch and we could hear muttering, but make out no words. He pulled the screen door open so forcefully after his conversation that I thought it would come off its hinges.

"Art," he said to his partner. "We gotta go. Sarge just got a call from a frantic parent that a kid was missing. They're right down the street."

Officer Hagerty finished taking our information, closed his book, and turned to join his partner, but not before I could see him raise his eyebrows in amazement. Before the door closed, Officer Podolsky turned back to us.

"Sorry, boys. I should have taken you more seriously. You've been a great help. Good work."

We looked at each other and then at Mr. Zalesky, who raised his can in salute.

●●●

Two days later I read the following in one of the daily newspapers that were delivered to our house:

*Yesterday, members of the Chicago Police Department raided James Robert Dawson's home on the 3200 block of North Campbell Avenue, recovering a seven-year-old boy who had been abducted the day before. The parents asked to keep the minor's name confidential. Officer Steven Podolsky credited information provided by two eyewitnesses to the abduction, both also minors, for the quick recovery of the kidnapped child. Also arrested at the home was Richard Dean Smith, allegedly a participant in the abduction.*

●●●

Mike hadn't seen the newspaper article, so I read it to him over the telephone.

"That's pretty cool, don't you think?" I said.

"Yeah, it is. I'm glad they were able to find the kid. Mostly, I'm glad they didn't print our names in the paper."

"Why?"

"Why?" he parroted. "Because people have forgotten what happened to us and I like it that way. I don't want to put up with any crap again."

"Yeah, you're right. I didn't even think about it," I admitted.

After a moment of silence, I said, "You know, what happened means that your ability hasn't gone away. So, maybe our radio signal theory is right."

"I thought about that, too, and I agree. That's really going to piss off Pete."

"It sure is," I agreed. "Have you heard from Pete lately?"

"Not for a couple of days. I wonder what's been going on with him and his mom."

"Me, too. Let's go over there tomorrow. Want to meet at ten o'clock?"

"Sure. See you then."

●●●

As planned, we met at Pete's house the next morning. Standing outside the door, it seemed eerily quiet.

"You feeling anything?" Mike said.

I closed my eyes, concentrated, and willed the door to magically disappear. When it didn't, I reached out and placed the palm of my right hand against the wood and waited.

"Mrs. Wilson is worried," I replied.

Mike nodded before knocking on the door. A moment later, Pete's mom opened the door and stared at us. A vacant stare. She said nothing.

"Hi, Mrs. Wilson. Can Pete come out?" I asked.

She looked at us and her expression made it seem as if she hadn't really noticed we were standing there until that very moment.

"Oh, hello boys." She joined us on the stoop, gently pulling the door mostly closed behind her. "I'm sorry. Pete's not well. The doctor gave him some medication, and he's sleeping. I don't want to wake him."

"What's wrong with him?" Mike asked.

"Well, boys, we don't really know. He had an episode yesterday."

Mike and I shared a quick glance before I said, "What kind of episode, Mrs. Wilson?"

"I don't rightly know, Jack. Something strange."

"Strange how, Mrs. Wilson?" Mike said.

"Well, we had to do some shopping. Clothes shopping. Otherwise, we would have just gone to the Jewel, like usual."

We waited for her to continue. I could feel her exhaustion and worry.

"OK," I prompted.

"Oh, sorry. We drove all the way to the other side of town. To Roosevelt Road, on the south side. We were on Lake Shore Drive, passing Grant Park, when Pete grabbed the sides of his head and shouted 'Make it stop.'"

Feigning innocence, Mike said, "Make what stop?"

"He said, 'Make the voices stop.'"

She shook, tears escaping and drawing lines in her makeup. "Oh boys, I'm so worried about him. He's hearing voices. I'm afraid he's becoming schizophrenic."

Neither of us knew what that meant, but we knew it wasn't good. We also knew we couldn't tell her anything we thought we might know.

She gathered herself and I could feel her dampen her fears. "Anyway, boys, I'll tell him you stopped by."

Simultaneously, we said, "Thank you."

As she turned to go back into the house, Mike said, "Would you tell him to call us, please? We're both worried."

She nodded and disappeared into her safe space.

●●●

To make sure Mrs. Wilson didn't catch a word, we put some distance between ourselves and Pete's, drifting toward Mike's house. When we thought we were sufficiently far enough from any prying ears, we stopped and sat on the curb.

"Holy moly! This is not good," I said.

"Not good at all," Mike agreed. "He really needs to get that under control."

"Yeah, but how?"

"I don't know."

We contemplated the predicament. Neither of us had a genius moment.

"What's a schizophrenic?" I said.

"No idea, but it doesn't sound good. We'll need to look it up in the dictionary."

"Yeah. So, what now?"

"I don't know. You want to come over to my house?"

There was nothing to do at my house and it was getting too cold to just hang around outside.

"Sure," I answered.

"Cool."

We pulled ourselves up from the curb and headed toward Mike's house. We hadn't gone far when a blue and white police car pulled next to us and stopped. The passenger side window rolled down and Officer Podolsky said, "Just the two I've been looking for."

I was puzzled as Mike and I approached the car.

"We haven't done anything, Officer," Mike offered.

Podolsky laughed. "Oh, yes you have, boys. You saved the life of one William Roberts. Little Billy's parents would like to meet you and say thanks." He motioned to the back seat with his head and said, "Climb on in."

•••

I felt awkward as we approached the Roberts' home. I could tell that Mike shared the feeling. Officers Podolsky and Hagerty hung back, letting Mike and me lead the way. Before we reached the door, the door flew open, someone flung aside the screen door, and a crying Mrs. Roberts bounded down the steps to intercept us. Her arms flung wide and she embraced us both, squeezing so hard it was difficult to breathe. Not knowing what else to do, I returned the embrace. I could see that Mike did the same.

After planting kisses on each of our cheeks, she said, "My two heroes. Thank you."

We stood in silence. I could feel the heat rising in my cheeks, a blush I couldn't control.

"Please come inside. I'd like you to meet Billy. He has something he'd like to say."

We followed her to the door, at which stood Mr. Roberts, looking distracted. Mrs. Roberts, who had until this point ignored her husband, said, "Honey, meet Jack and Mike."

He held his hand out and said, "Thank you, boys. That was a great thing you did."

We each shook his hand before entering the house. Not sure what to do, I turned to Officer Podolsky, a questioning look etched upon my face.

"Go ahead, guys. We'll wait out here for you."

Following Mrs. Roberts, we went into the kitchen, where hot

chocolate and home-baked chocolate chip cookies waited. Also waiting was seven-year-old Billy. Upon seeing us, he hurried forward, held his hand out, and said, "Thank you for what you did, Jack and Mike. I will be forever grateful."

We each shook his outstretched hand and muttered our thanks. I could feel Mrs. Robert's pride at her son having performed just as they'd rehearsed.

"Please, sit down. I baked these cookies just for you."

She poured cups of hot cocoa for each of us and placed a couple of cookies on plates, placing one in front of each of us. As Mr. Roberts entered the room, I could feel her nervous energy ramp up. He was cold. Not physically, but emotionally. As if he had better things to do and more important places to be.

As we ate and drank, she prattled. I nodded here and there where it seemed appropriate, Mike following my lead. Finally, it was time to leave. She gave each of us another hug and again said, "Thank you."

"We're glad we could help," Mike said.

She beamed a smile in our direction before Mr. Roberts led us to the door. Without a word, he opened the door and delivered us to the waiting police officers.

In the backseat of the squad car once again, I whispered to Mike, "That was weird."

He nodded, never taking his eyes off the police officers.

When we arrived at Mike's house, Officer Hagerty pulled over to the curb, and Officer Podolsky got out to open the back door for us. It wasn't that he was acting as our servant. It was because the back doors of police cars didn't open from the inside.

"Thanks for doing that, guys. It meant a lot to Mrs. Roberts. You boys take care now."

As the police cruiser pulled away, I was still trying to process the different emotions that had bombarded me at the Roberts' house.

# CHAPTER 12
# THOSE ARE SOME BIG WORDS

It had been two days since we knocked on Pete's door, and I still hadn't heard from him. Neither had Mike. I was worried. My mom was in her usual position on the couch, watching some soap opera. I took a chance and dialed Pete's telephone number.

"Hello."

I was so surprised I couldn't answer for a moment. "Pete, is that you?"

"Hey, Jack. How you doing?"

I stretched out the eight-foot-long cord and entered the small bathroom around the corner from the kitchen, closing the door softly on the cord. I often used this as my personal phone booth in an attempt at privacy.

"Hey, Pete. I'm good. Did your mom tell you that Mike and I stopped over to see you the other day?"

"Yeah, she did. They've got me taking some kind of medication that makes me really sleepy."

"How are you feeling otherwise?"

"OK, I guess," he said.

"Your mom said you heard loud voices when you drove by

Grant Park. What happened?"

"Just that. We were driving. I was looking out the window, and suddenly my head was filled with voices. Voices in pain. It took me totally by surprise."

"Oh, man. Did you try to block them out at all?"

"Geez, Jack, it happened so fast I didn't have time to think." He paused, gathering his thoughts. "I know I should have tried, but once they were in my head, I couldn't do anything but scream. I'm sorry."

"That's OK. I just wanted to be sure you weren't sick."

"I have a doctor's appointment tomorrow, but I feel pretty good. Except for being tired from the medicine. What have you guys been up to?"

I filled him in on how we thwarted the kidnapping, recounted our run-in with the police, and shared the details of our meeting with Billy and his parents.

"Oh, man. That's amazing! You two are like actual heroes. I wish I could have been there."

"So do we."

"Yeah. Although there's not much my hearing voices would've helped you with."

There wasn't much I could have said, so I changed the subject.

"Be sure to call after your doctor's appointment. Hopefully, your mom will let you out soon."

"Yeah, I hope so. Later."

"Later."

I disconnected the call and sat alone in my private phone booth. I had no idea what the doctors would come up with, but I had a bad feeling about it, nonetheless.

●●●

Talking to Pete reminded me to look up schizophrenic in the dictionary:

*A person with schizophrenia.*

Since I had no idea what schizophrenia was, the definition was of no help. I let my finger slide up and down the page until I found it:

*A mental illness that is characterized by disturbances in thought (such as delusions), perception (such as hallucinations), and behavior (such as disorganized speech or catatonic behavior), by a loss of emotional responsiveness and extreme apathy, and by noticeable deterioration in the level of functioning in everyday life.*

Wow, that was a lot of big words—most of them went over my head. The only part I really got was *mental illness*, and that alone scared me.

Now I really had a bad feeling about what was happening with Pete.

# INTERLUDE #1

The world was a billion years old when Earth first entered the orbit of the Sun. It formed from matter scattered through its universe by an explosion that would have consumed the Milky Way, forming a planet made from rock, energy, dark matter, and stardust. It spent an eon aimlessly wandering its universe, guided by random violent meetings with other debris of the same explosion, until it came upon a giant white star. Its speed at the time of the meeting was such that it shot past the star, seemingly without slowing. As it passed, solar flares scorched its surface and penetrated deep inside its crust, bringing it unexpectedly to life. Slowly, the gravitational field of the star wrapped its tentacles around the world, gently slowing it and placing it in orbit almost one hundred million miles away.

●●●

While the planet originally had a hard metal core, the solar flares melted the material, set it spinning, and caused the liquid metal to balloon. The expansion caused earthquakes and volcanic eruptions, and left a portion of the enlarged core chamber empty, inviting it to be filled by the vast store of pure energy which made up the planet. The energy, crackling and humming with power, filled not only the chamber, but the vast network of fissures and tunnels throughout the world.

The first life forms emerged countless millennia before man or woman. They coalesced from the ingredients that came together to form the world. Their first physical form was helpless, microscopic, and without predators, allowing them to grow and flourish. The energy of the planet flowed through their physical form.

Over time, these life forms evolved into intelligent, bipedal beings with a visceral connection to their world. Other life forms that inhabited the land, seas, air, and underground portions of the world joined them.

Fueled by the energy coursing through their bodies and forming a direct connection with their world, they rapidly developed large brains and an insatiable appetite for knowledge. Technology quickly advanced, allowing them to explore not only their world but also other worlds of their universe. They developed the means to travel vast distances in short periods of time, feeding on the available energy. Their existence was peaceful and fulfilling, allowing them time to further expand their technology and quench their thirst for knowledge.

Then they became bored.

# PART TWO

# ALL GROWN UP

# <u>PETE</u>

## CHAPTER 13
## AN UNHEALTHY OBSESSION

My name is Peter Wilson. Everybody calls me Pete. When I was ten-years-old, I had three days of my life stolen. Now, fifty years later, I still did not know who, or what, had taken them or where I had been. Although I have no memory of what happened during that time, those three missing days sure shaped the rest of my life.

•••

1969 and 1970 were years that really sucked. In 1969, my father died. In 1970, as I said, I disappeared for three days. I wasn't alone. My so-called best friends, Jack and Mike, were with me. We were riding our bicycles, and the next thing we knew, we were in the hospital, where doctors went to town doing tests, and the police treated us like suspects instead of victims. When neither the doctors nor the cops could figure anything out, they let us go home.

Besides the odd white streak in our hair—a mark I've come to see as a brand—we were unchanged from who we were before we vanished. And we pretty much were. The same as before, I mean. None of us felt any different, even if a lot of other people looked at us as freaks.

Then something happened. Not to us, but more with us.

Let me explain. We were discovered in our favorite park. Since we practically lived there, returning after the hospital was natural. We rode our bikes toward the place where they found us. That's when I heard voices. None of the other guys heard them. They were in my head. It sounded like screaming and pleading and freaked the shit out of me. Mike said he felt what he called the evil of the place, whatever that meant. Jack seemed unaffected, although I learned he could suddenly feel other people's emotions. Whatever.

My thought process was pretty much, "What the fuck!?!" The others thought we should try to get what they called our new abilities under control. When they said that, it made sense, even though it still freaked me out. So, we went to a couple of places Mike had been and felt the supposed evil. Like I said, it seemed to make sense at the time.

When we arrived at the places Mike had led us to, the voices were there, but quiet. I convinced myself that I was losing my ability to hear voices, and I couldn't have been happier. Mike could barely feel the evil, so I thought he, too, was losing his ability. Jack was still capable of feeling the emotions of others, or so he said. I'm still not sure what that even meant. Anyway, we spent some time trying to control what we could, none of us being very successful. Over the next few weeks, we returned to those places, each time the voices and feeling of evil being less and less. I was certain that I had lost any trace of being able to hear them, which brightened my day.

A few weeks later, while Jack and Mike played at being

heroes for witnessing a kidnapping, I had to go clothes shopping with my mom. We drove down Lake Shore Drive to the south side of the city. LSD, as it's known to the locals, is just what it sounds like: a road that follows Lake Michigan towards downtown. Beaches lined one side of the road, while vast park areas were on the other. It was always beautiful, and I enjoyed the views. Until my head exploded with the sound of voices. Voices in pain. Pleading voices. It caught me so by surprise that I screamed out and grabbed the sides of my head. I definitely scared the crap out of my mother, who nearly swerved into the lane next to us, causing a loud and long honking horn to join the noise already filling my head.

She got off LSD at the next exit, found a place to pull over, and asked what the hell was wrong. All I could say was, "Make it stop! Make the voices stop!"

Had I been thinking more clearly, I probably wouldn't have said what I did. But, it was out and I couldn't unsay it. The look of concern on my mother's face told me all I needed to know about what would happen next. The shopping trip was over as she got back on LSD, going in the opposite direction towards home.

●●●

Doctors. My next few days were consumed by doctors. Of course, that early on, they couldn't really make an accurate diagnosis, so they fed me pills that made it impossible to do anything but sleep. For days. When they stopped feeding me the pills, it was time for more doctors, this time of the psychiatric kind. My mother kept throwing around her own diagnoses, using words like psychotic and schizophrenic, although I'm convinced she had no real idea what those meant or looked like in real life and not on television.

Shortly after that incident, I began therapy. In 1970, therapy wasn't something people bragged about. Quite the contrary. It was a secret. A shameful thing to be hidden from everybody. Of course, I had to tell Jack and Mike, but that's only because I knew they'd keep it quiet.

My therapist, or more accurately, my psychiatrist, Dr. Goldman, a well-meaning but clueless fifty-four-year-old man, average in every way, worked through his checklist of causes for auditory hallucinations. And man, what a checklist it was. Alcoholism, dementia, brain tumor, drug abuse, epilepsy, hearing loss, infections, stress, mental illness, migraines, Parkinson's disease, sleep issues, thyroid disease, and even tinnitus. The list went on forever, and getting through it took many months. Finally, he narrowed it down to mental illness or stress. It took a while, but he finally asked the question I knew was inevitable: "When did you start hearing voices?"

The next few sessions dealt with my disappearance and when I heard voices. He asked whether Jack and/or Mike heard voices, to which I could honestly answer in the negative. He didn't ask if they had any other strange effects, so I didn't volunteer any information about them.

I was honest with the doctor when it came to what I heard and when I heard it. And, I could report that since the occurrence on Lake Shore Drive months before, I hadn't experienced the voices. I was certain he was going to announce that it was all psychosomatic and related to the stress of having disappeared.

That's when it happened. During a session in his office, things were going well, with nothing out of the ordinary. I was about to tell him something inconsequential when my hands flew to my ears and I screamed. It was involuntary, like flinching when someone tries to kick you in the balls. I ran to the window, looking for a reason, any reason, for the sudden attack. All I saw was a park. A green expanse filled with kids playing.

"Fuck!"

Dr. Goldman quickly moved to my side, trying to see what I saw. When nothing was visible except the park, he led me back to my chair, where I sat with my ears covered, rocked back and forth, and muttered, "Shut up! Shut up!"

Out came the notepad, and he was off, jotting things down while I just sat there, miserable. I looked up and saw him talking, but I had no idea what he was saying. Everything was muffled, except the sounds in my head. He came to my chair and shook me, his face directly in front of mine, shouting my name. After an interminable time, the voices faded, and I could hear him once again.

"Tell me what happened."

I did.

So much for my psychosomatic diagnosis. He immediately went to the next most obvious choice. Mental illness. What kind was yet to be determined, but he viewed the occurrence as a great breakthrough. An opportunity to really get this thing figured out.

Lucky him.

This was early in the "better living through chemistry" era, so it was time to prescribe more drugs. The newer and more experimental, the better. The first was Haldol. As I heard the doctor explain to my mother, it blocked dopamine receptors in the brain, stopping the symptoms. Neither she nor I had any idea what that meant, but she was willing to give anything a try. Or rather, she was willing for *me* to give anything a try. So that's what we did.

●●●

I was still in school, trying to keep a low profile. The white streak in my hair didn't help, so I tried dying it the same color as my other hair. It didn't work. So, with my unique identifying mark, the drugs, and the side effects, which included jerky, involuntary motions of my head, neck, arms, and body, a low profile was difficult. School is a hard enough social environment without standing out as a freak, and even if others didn't view me that way, I couldn't help but think of myself like that. I stayed on the Haldol for weeks, but when my breasts swelled, I decided I'd had enough and stopped taking it. I didn't tell anybody about that decision, including my mother, and, after about a week, felt more like myself than I had in a long time. Unfortunately for me, after I'd been off the medication for about a month, Dr. Goldman drew some blood and ran some tests. The jig was up. I explained why I'd stopped, so, instead of just letting me be, he thought a different drug would be in order. This time it was Thorazine. The wonderful array of side effects, which are similar to Haldol's side effects, included weight gain, insomnia, and an almost total loss of my personality. Once again, after a month, I stopped taking the drug, feeling better shortly thereafter. Dr. Goldman didn't like it, but I'd threatened my mother with telling people about my therapy and drug taking. She wasn't willing to face the humiliation, so backed me up with the good doctor. Therapy, however, continued.

And for quite a while, I didn't experience the voices.

●●●

Jack and Mike tried to be supportive. I know they did. But I couldn't help but be pissed that I was the only one having to go through this. It affected our relationship, which, now, I can own up to. That didn't change the fact that we shared a bond, but I also couldn't stop myself from pushing them away. It was gradual, but continuous.

I became afraid to travel outside known territories and avoided large open spaces whenever possible. I used this as an excuse to avoid going anywhere with them. Even when it came to riding our bikes to the beach, something I'd always loved.

My world became ruled by fear.

I tried to convince myself that the voices had gone for good. Every time I did that, I'd have a surprise somewhere. It always caught me off guard, so I always had the same reaction. And it didn't matter how old I was. I never got used to it and I never learned to control it.

I found myself alone, even when surrounded by those I had considered to be friends. After a particularly strong and disturbing episode, I confessed to both my mother and Dr. Goldman that I was still hearing the voices, which led to the reintroduction of medication. Which led to more side effects, which led to depression, which led to the most shameful of all possibilities.

Suicide.

●●●

More accurately, attempted suicide, as I am obviously not dead. Yet.

This was in 1977, when I was still a minor and subject to the life-changing decisions of my mother. With the help of the good doctor, she had me involuntarily committed as a threat to myself or others. And that's how I came to find myself at the Elgin Mental Health Center in glorious Elgin, Illinois. Actually, I prefer its original name, the Northern Illinois Hospital and Asylum for the Insane, but staff frowned at its use.

It opened in 1872, and, as you might imagine, looked just as one would think a nineteenth-century asylum would look. It was large and imposing and terribly under-funded. The best thing about it, from my point of view, was that it was in a city and not bordering any large parks.

●●●

My therapy continued, but at some point, I realized it was all for naught. I wasn't going to get better, whatever that meant. Whatever had happened to me during those missing three days was responsible for my ability to hear the voices. A more curious person might have wanted to delve into that. Me, I just took my medication and let nature and time take its course. I slept a lot and felt my personality slipping away. What they called institutional syndrome. It allowed me to let go of personal responsibility for anything. I stopped living and merely existed.

I was fine with that.

My mother, however, let it eat away at her soul. She neglected herself, and doctors diagnosed her with ovarian cancer. She stopped coming to visit and died in 1990, leaving me with the soul-crushing burden of having shamed her to death.

As had become my motto over the years, I simply said, "Fuck it," and took more medication.

●●●

In 2008, they tore down many of the older asylum buildings

and replaced them with new, modern structures. I suppose it was an improvement, except for one thing. The powers-that-be decided the campus needed more open green spaces. Yep, the one thing the place had going for it, at least from my perspective, was gone. My anxiety levels rose, and in group therapy, I confessed my fears. That led to more medication. I was losing myself. If I wasn't mentally ill when I got here, I certainly was by now.

●●●

I'd been in here so long my mind was turning to mush. The side effects of my medications made it impossible to do anything about it. I was content in my lethargy, willing to let others perform as many of my daily functions as they were being paid to perform. Time to eat? Just lead me to my table. Time for therapy? Take me to the right room and sit me in a chair. Time for a shower? No problem, as long as you can get me there, undressed, dried off, and redressed.

I spent a lot of time looking out the window of my room at the newly opened green space. Maybe it was boredom. Maybe it was paranoia. Maybe it was a combination. Did I hear voices as I stared out the window? I couldn't be sure. Sometimes it seemed I did, but my senses were so dulled it was hard to make out. And what if I did? What could I do about it? Not a damn thing. What could I do about anything? That's right. Not a damn thing.

It had taken years, but I was getting angry. I was too drugged to display any aggression, but man, could I internalize. I was pissed at hearing voices. I was pissed at being locked away. I was pissed about having my life stolen. I was pissed at Jack. I was pissed at Mike.

Fuckin Jack. Fuckin Mike.

●●●

I've been in here for what, over forty years? In all that time, I've heard from Jack and Mike a handful of times, all early in my stay. What the hell!?! I thought we said we'd stick together, but I guess that meant only when it was convenient. OK, so I didn't make much of an effort either, but really, let's compare circumstances. Where were they? Where are they? I bet they've forgotten all about me while they're out there living their lives. Actual lives.

Bastards.

●●●

I wonder if they ever think about me. I think about them. All the time. Even in my current state, I know it's an unhealthy obsession.

Do they have wives? Girlfriends? Wives and girlfriends? Kids? Jobs? All the things I should've had.

Are they happy? Do I want them to be happy or to suffer? I think I want them to suffer in their happiness.

Am I jealous? Envious? Pissed?

Is it hate or love? Can it be both?

Man, am I fucked up, or what?

Damn them.

Fuck it. I'm over it.

# <u>MIKE</u>

## CHAPTER 14
## TUPELO HONEY

My name is Mike Plotkin. When I was ten-years-old, I went missing for three days. I'm sixty-years-old now and no closer to knowing what happened then when I was ten. Whatever it was, it sent me down a life path, for better or worse.

●●●

I had just turned ten-years-old when my mother died. It wasn't easy on me, my dad, and my older brother, Zach. Zach was four years older than me and, in 1970, in the throes of teenage rebellion. Without our mother to ride herd on him, Zach quickly became out of control. My dad did what he could, which wasn't much. He was in mourning and trying to keep his shit together while not losing his job and raising his boys. I think it was toughest for Dad. He was of the generation in which the woman stayed home and took care of the house and kids while the man worked to provide enough money for the wife to do those things. Mom's death left my father lost. He had no idea about running a household or raising kids, especially boys. He firmly believed in the "boys will be boys" philosophy, so he gave us free rein. I think it was just easier for him not to deal with us while he tried to figure out the rest of his life. Looking back, I'm fairly certain that meant finding a new wife.

Zach took full advantage of the situation. Consequently, I encountered marijuana, hashish, LSD (not the road in Chicago), and various other popular drugs of that era, thanks to Zach. Exposed not in that I did any of those, but I was a witness to his experimentation. I learned valuable life lessons from his mistakes. I have to admit, however, that the music he exposed me to was, and still is, the best of all time.

With everything that Zach and my dad had going on, and there being no female presence in the house, there wasn't a lot of conversation to be had. We rarely ate meals together, and when we did, the conversation usually centered on either the Cubs, Bears, or Blackhawks, the three major Chicago sports teams of the day. Superficial at best. I didn't experience the deep bonding that a death in the family sometimes provides. If conversation is an art, it was not an art being taught at the school of hard knocks in session at the Plotkin residence. I'm pretty certain that's why I have always been a man of few words and little outward emotion. More than once in my life, I've been described as being taciturn, a description with which I can't really argue.

Not having any close relationships at home, I found what solace and friendship I could with my two best buds, Jack and Pete. We each shared the bond of having recently lost a family member and having to deal with a fucked-up home life. We naturally gravitated towards one another, even before tragedy struck. It was the shared tragedy that cemented the bond. We did everything we could together. We practically lived outside, riding our bikes seemingly everywhere, not bound by the invisible tendrils of cellphones and GPS trackers.

•••

It was while the three of us were together riding our bikes through our home-away-from-home, Rogers Park, that the life-altering event occurred. Maybe not life-altering, but definitely life-defining. Who knows what life would have been without it? Maybe not that much different, although I don't really believe that.

We were racing to get Pete home so he could help his mom. I remember feeling great, riding with total abandon. Then I remember waking up in the hospital. Nothing between those two events. A total void in my memory. In my life.

The doctors were baffled. Except for an inexplicable white streak in my hair, there didn't appear to be any difference between the last day I remembered and waking in the hospital. I felt fine. Strong even. That didn't stop the doctors from doing a complete battery of tests, with my father's permission, of course. My father's generation had learned from their parents that doctors were not to be questioned. If they ordered a test, the test was to be administered. They went on for days.

In between testing came the questioning. The working theory was that we had to have been abducted. It made sense, even to us kids. We were questioned separately and together.

There was Good Cop and Bad Cop. It was like watching a shitty police procedural on television. They even went so far as to hook us up to a lie detector machine. When the results came back showing that I, and presumably my friends, had told the truth, the police were at a dead end. When the medical tests showed we hadn't been drugged and had no physical injuries, the doctors joined the police at their dead end. Ultimately, they had no choice but to cut us loose.

●●●

Shortly after being released from the hospital, things took a strange turn. Boys being boys, we thought it would be a good idea to visit the location where we had been found. I believe my father described it as our having been "spat from the ground" and left to be found. In my mind, we were going to undertake our own investigation. If someone had found us in the open, some evidence must have been left behind that the police missed. We couldn't have actually been "spat from the ground." There had to be tracks of some sort. Nobody could have carried the three of us and our bikes without leaving some evidence. A vehicle must have been used to transport us, most likely a big car with a large trunk. Which meant almost all the cars in the neighborhood. Back then, a pickup truck in the city was not a common sight, and someone would surely have remembered seeing one drive onto the grass. So, in my mind, there had to be tire tracks waiting to be discovered and run through some secret law enforcement database.

We approached the site with caution, my eyes scanning for

tire impressions. I was just turning my head to scan a different area when I felt something strange. It didn't touch me physically, but it hit a part of my brain I hadn't even known was there. It was like my fight-or-flight reflex got supercharged—shocked awake and roaring to life. The hackles on the back of my neck felt like porcupine quills, while at the same time, Robot from *Lost in Space* had taken up residency in my head, screaming "Danger Mike Plotkin! Danger! Danger!" I stopped in my tracks. At the same time, I heard actual screaming and turned in the direction from which it emanated to see Pete holding his hands over his ears and yelling, "Make it stop!" Or something like that.

I made my way to Pete and, together with Jack, we moved him away from the site until he could remove his hands from his head and stop shouting.

Afterwards, we made our way to a local hot dog joint, where we talked about the experience. It was there I first learned of Jack's ability to feel the emotions of others.

●●●

Our ten-year-old brains were working overtime to come to grips with what was happening to us. Jack and I thought it would make sense to learn about these abilities and get them under control. Pete was prepared to ignore it and hope it was a one-off experience. Jack and I prevailed, and we undertook what I thought of as training exercises.

We waited a while before starting practice. We only knew of one place where the abilities had been triggered: where we had been found, in Rogers Park. So, after what we thought would be a reasonable period of time to get our courage up, we went back. Cautiously. I was surprised at how faintly my warning mechanism was working. Pete said the voices were almost imperceptible.

Now what?

A short while later, while in the car with my dad, I had the warning experience multiple times. Twice, I received warnings at parks, but once, the warning clearly targeted a person. Yet another new experience I had no idea what to make of.

I suggested to the guys that if we were really going to practice getting ourselves under control, we needed to go to one or both parks. Once again, Pete was reluctant, but came along anyway.

To make a long story short, it went much better for me and Jack than it did for Pete. He just wouldn't, or couldn't, get control of the voices. They always startled and scared him, even if he knew they were coming. I lied about having any control—just so he wouldn't feel worse. I'm sure Jack was pretending too.

●●●

Sometime later, Jack and I were leaving Rogers Park and, while crossing a neighborhood street, my brain once again screamed, "Danger Mike Plotkin! Danger! Danger!" I stopped in my tracks, right in the middle of the street, where

Jack and I stood frozen and witnessed a kidnapping. In broad daylight! We ran to a nearby house and convinced the owner to call the police. Using the information we provided, the victim, a little boy, was located a lot faster than would have otherwise been possible.

I didn't know it then, but that experience would shape my adult life.

More on that later.

●●●

By the time I was seventeen, I had experienced inner warnings more times than I could count. Those places were usually open spaces, like where they had found us in 1970, but not always. As time passed, I increasingly realized that "evil" could be found anywhere and everywhere. Out of necessity and self-preservation, I became very adept at controlling my reactions and dampening the alarm bells in my head. Aside from Pete and Jack, nobody knew my secret. When I heard what happened to Pete, I became even more obsessed with maintaining complete secrecy.

Pete hadn't ever been able to get the voice hearing thing under control. It always caught him by surprise, and his reaction was always the same. His mother enrolled him in therapy, and doctors heavily medicated him for extended periods. At seventeen years old, he attempted suicide. He stockpiled pills during periods when he stopped taking his medication. It didn't matter what they were or what they were intended to do. One day, I think after another episode of voices, he downed whatever he could of his stockpile and lay on his bed. Hours later, his mother came to check on him and found him unconscious, empty pill bottles lying haphazardly in his room. Using the newly authorized 911 emergency number saved his life. Based on the fact that he's been in an institution since then, I'm not so certain that was a good thing.

I often wondered if there was anything I could have done to help with Pete's situation. Jack and I both tried to help him control the voices, or at least his reaction to them, but he just couldn't get it. I think he had convinced himself it would fade with time and he'd be fine. So much for wishful thinking. Over time, even though I tried to keep in touch, he stopped responding, choosing to let the friendship die on the vine. Regardless, I still feel a special affinity for Pete. We shared too much to ever forget.

●●●

I wasn't one of those people who knew what they wanted to do with their life from an early age. If I had been a musical or scientific prodigy, a path would have been laid open before me. It would have only required taking steps to follow it. For those of us who didn't fall into the prodigy category of anything that could prove useful in life experience, deciding at age seventeen or eighteen what to do with the rest of your life was daunting. If I were totally honest, it would have to be described as terrifying. How could we be expected to know at that stage of life? What experiences did we really have to draw on? Partying and trying to get laid didn't really qualify as career paths. Yet, we faced decisions impacting our lives in ways we couldn't comprehend.

Guidance counselors. Our high school had them, although only a small percentage of students actually took them seriously. I have to say that I was not among that small percentage. However, we were required to schedule at least three sessions with them during our junior year, so I did.

●●●

Ms. Tupelo was in her late twenties, with long blonde hair and a terrific body. She could have been the poster woman for the hippie movement, had she only worn a flower in her hair. The spitting image of the actress on that television show, The Mod Squad. She embodied the stuff of fantasy. Every time I said her name, in my mind I had to add "Honey" afterward. A silent homage to Van Morrison.

During our first session, we went through the typical questions: "What are you interested in? Is there anything you think you'd enjoy doing? Is there a family business that interests you?"

Already mostly being the taciturn person I would become, my answers were short. Curt. I knew I was wasting the time of both of us and couldn't wait to get out of there. The second session was almost identical to the first, until she said, "So, Mike, I'm trying to understand you a little better. Tell me why you dyed that streak in your hair."

The question took me so by surprise that I responded

honestly. "I didn't dye it." She didn't need to be a trained professional to notice how uncomfortable the question had made me.

"Oh, so you were born with it? How interesting."

I had known someone who had been born with an interesting star pattern in his hair, so it was a possibility. And I could have just let it go at that. I could have, but didn't.

"No, I wasn't born with it. It happened when I was ten." I made a show of checking the time and said, "I really have to go. I'll see you next week."

I was up and out of the door before she had an opportunity to respond.

●●●

When I arrived for what was to be our final session, I noticed a larger-than-usual file on her desk. As I sat in the waiting chair, she opened the file and flipped through its pages.

"Hey Mike," she said, without looking up. "After our last meeting, my curiosity became piqued, so I did some research." She looked up, locking eyes. "That must have been a very traumatic time, when you were ten."

I maintained eye contact, but said nothing as I slouched in the seat, fulfilling my role as the taciturn teenager.

Turning her attention back to the file, she continued. "I also see that when you were ten, you witnessed a kidnapping." Turning her attention back to me, she said, "Tell me about that."

I recounted the tale in as much detail as possible. With the retelling, I became more engaged, sitting upright and becoming more animated. When I finished the telling, all the way through having been brought to meet little Billy and his parents, it was as if I had become a different person.

"How'd that make you feel, Mike?"

For the first time during one of our sessions, I gave a question real consideration. "You know, it made me feel great. Probably better than anything else had." It was a realization I had not come to before that very moment.

She closed the file, and I could see how pleased she was. "I think we may have just stumbled upon something, Mike."

I thought so, too, but was clueless as to what it might have been.

"Have you ever given any thought to a career in law enforcement?"

I hadn't. Not until that very instant.

Bless you, Ms. Tupelo.

(Honey).

# CHAPTER 15
# HARD DECISIONS

Having some direction in my life made an enormous difference for me, from a mental standpoint. I knew how having contributed to the recovery of little Billy made me feel. What had led me to be in the position to witness the kidnapping was also apparent: my internal evil warning system. I thought about how Pete had let what happened get the better of him. I determined to use my "gift" to forge a career and help others.

I studied criminal justice at the University of Illinois and, immediately upon graduation, applied to the Federal Bureau of Investigation. My evil warning system, I was sure, would give me the upper hand in identifying and locating the perpetrators of crime. I wasn't wrong. What I was wrong about was thinking it would be easy just because I had that advantage. While I could quickly zero in on a suspect, the real challenge came afterward—digging into the investigation was time-consuming and draining. Although I was mostly able to control the strength and effect of my warning moments, what I could never control was my personal connection and involvement in my cases, especially when they involved children. I obsessed. My mind would not shut off. The mental toll proved to be physically debilitating.

●●●

While in college, I met a wonderful woman, Wendy. We met in an English course, and the attraction was immediate. English was not a focus for me, but was one of those required courses that had to be checked off the list in order to get a degree. Wendy took it much more seriously than I did and excelled. We stayed together through college and got married right after my admission to the FBI.

The adage that opposites attract certainly proved to be true in our case. We loved each other, of that I was certain, but her thought processes and mine didn't really mesh. As a law enforcement officer, I entered a conservative, by-the-book environment. She entered the business world and moved up the ladder. A world of money, social functions, and snobbery. I don't think there's a word that encompasses my level of discomfort with that world. The same can probably be said for her comfort level within my world.

When I became involved in a case, it would take over my life. Every aspect. I was gone, both mentally and physically, for long stretches of time. Marriage shouldn't be a lonely endeavor, yet that's exactly what it became for Wendy.

We divorced after five years of marriage. I wished her the best and meant every word.

●●●

During my tenure at the FBI, the bureau assigned me to various field offices. Since my specialty was serial killers and abductions, the posts were usually in larger cities. Which made perfect sense. Unfortunately for me, it meant I was constantly being bombarded by warning signals in my brain. Even though I had learned to mostly control them, the relentless barrage eventually got to me.

Still, I loved the work I was doing. The feeling of having saved someone from a horrific fate was like adrenalin to an adrenalin junkie. The wins happened far less often than I had hoped, but the scarcity made each one that much sweeter. Any win always brought me back to the day of Billy Roberts' kidnapping, my first taste of victory over evil.

That quest for victory became the driving force of my life. My case load was much larger than it should have been due to my inability to say "No." I thought I should have been able to save them all, and over time, became consumed by the failures. I knew it was part of the job, but still couldn't help but take it all personally.

I faced hard choices. Hoping against all hope to overcome the inevitable, I could continue on. I could blow my brains out. Or, I could take an early retirement and move to a small, isolated community. I wish I could say I hadn't really considered putting a gun in my mouth, but that wouldn't be truthful. I had considered it on more than one occasion. Maybe it was cowardice. I don't know. I finally chose the early retirement route.

Hard decision having been made, I executed the plan. Not really having any idea where to move, I put a map on the wall and a pin in my hand. Eyes closed, I moved forward, arm outstretched and pin at the ready, eager to find my new home. The pin went in, I opened my eyes, and took a step back.

Big Sky, Montana.

# <u>JACK</u>

## CHAPTER 16
## DRIFTING

This is Jack Winterhaven. As I had previously mentioned, when I was ten-years-old, I disappeared for three days. Now, fifty years later, despite that experience having opened opportunities I would not have otherwise been aware of, I finally came to grips with the fact I'd probably never know what really happened.

●●●

So, how to continue? Maybe with drifting. As in drifting apart. Pete, Mike, and I were as thick as thieves, as the saying goes. Grief and an unexplained disappearance drew us together and bonded our friendship. I thought that whatever it was we had been through, it would keep us together in friendship, regardless of what the future might hold. I guess it just goes to show how naïve I was.

●●●

The shared experience of witnessing the kidnapping of Billy Roberts had profound effects on both Mike and me. I know it was the reason Mike went into law enforcement. As for me, it opened my eyes to the emotions felt by two people in a marriage.

I was still adjusting to being able to feel the emotional states of others. I had never been very adept at feeling even my own emotions, so this new experience was quite jarring. When I had been in the Roberts' home, I felt the husband's coldness and the wife's trepidation in his presence. Having never felt anything quite like it, I determined to pay attention when in the presence of married people. To my surprise, those feelings were more common than I had thought possible. The more I considered, the more curious I became. It got me wondering about my own parents and what their relationship had been like. Had there ever been a time when they were happy? There must have been. I recalled a time when I was about four or so and walked into their bedroom. The door was open, so it wasn't like I was interrupting them. But I saw what to me was the strangest thing I'd ever seen: my father with his arm around my mother, and her snuggled up to him. Even at four years old, I was speechless. I had never seen them do anything but fight. I just turned away and went back to my room. So, even in their marriage, there must have been some level of happiness, fleeting though it might have been.

As time went on and I progressed through the school system, a decision confronted me. What did I want to do with the rest of my life? My first thought was, *I'm only seventeen years old. How the fuck am I supposed to know?* I was well aware that such thinking wouldn't help, but come on, I *was* only seventeen. Then, as is so often the case, when I wasn't thinking about it, I remembered Mr. and Mrs. Roberts and all of those other unhappily married couples. I thought that my ability to know what the truthful emotions of these people were should allow me to cut through the bullshit and offer a real chance at helping. And just like that, I made the decision that would guide the rest of my life.

●●●

Pete's attempted suicide gutted me. I could feel his despair, but the medication he was so often taking masked the depth. I felt guilt. Why, I couldn't say. Only that the guilt was present then and remains to this day. Knowing there was nothing I could have done, and having the professional training I have, made no difference. A level of guilt still persisted. I think the feeling of guilt was exacerbated by the fact that Pete pulled away from me and Mike. It's my belief that he somehow held me, and probably Mike, responsible for his plight. Not rational, but maybe he was not in a rational place. Could I have been more persistent in my attempts at keeping in touch? Probably. Could Pete have put forth any effort? Maybe, maybe not. If there's fault to be placed, I'll take it. I'm not the one being held in confinement and being fed drugs. So, yeah. I'll take it.

●●●

My ability had led me to discover that my mother and uncle had not always been truthful with me. On more than one occasion he had supposedly taken my mother shopping, only to be gone way too long. There was always a readily available bullshit excuse, but I knew. After the fourth such excursion, I privately confronted my uncle. He could tell I knew something was going on and swore me to secrecy, as my mother didn't want me to worry.

The "shopping" outings were actually doctor appointments. She hadn't been feeling well, and her drinking hadn't subsided. I had noticed what I thought was a deterioration in her health, but did not know to what extent. She had the trifecta of death: cirrhosis of the liver, heart disease, and lung cancer. The only question was, which would kill her first?

And the winner was…heart disease. The stress of her other diseases, combined with her drinking, was just too much, and her heart gave out just after my high school graduation. The house was paid off by her old life insurance policy, which meant I had a place to stay. But even with the practicalities taken care of, the emptiness she left behind was impossible to ignore.

●●●

Since I had a place to live, it made sense for me to go to college locally. Because of my "unfortunate circumstances," I qualified for financial aid and, together with my part-time job, was able to attend and pay for classes at DePaul University, where I met my future bride, Anna.

We had a small wedding, with only immediate family and close friends in attendance. Mike was there. I am sorry to say that it was one of the last times we were together.

●●●

So the drifting of the three young best friends had been completed. Mike and I each had our separate lives and professions, while Pete remained in the asylum.

Life is so strange.

# CHAPTER 17
# REVELATION

It's strange how something that once seemed so traumatic and life-threatening could turn out to be such a blessing. At least for me.

If it hadn't been for that three-day disappearance and the resultant ability to read the emotions of others, I'm not sure what direction my life would have taken. The direction was certainly surprising to me. I'm not someone who particularly enjoyed school. So, choosing a profession in which not only a college degree but an advanced Master's Degree was required was not something I would otherwise have planned. But I had a goal and determination, which, I discovered, went a long way in overcoming my dislike of institutional learning.

●●●

Anna was in the nursing program at DePaul and used to go to the library for a quiet place to study. Even though I had a house in which to study, I also went to the library for the same purpose. At home, there were just too many distractions, both real and imagined. The stereo beckoned, the television teased, and the refrigerator would constantly call my name. I may have had a goal and determination, but discipline was a different matter. At the library, I could insert earplugs, grab a cubicle, and bury my face in a book, pretending I was totally alone. Which usually worked.

Usually.

One day, I was in my pretend bubble when someone walked by, stopped, and came back to my chair, not saying anything, but waiting for me to notice. Which I did. It was a very attractive girl, a little older than me, I thought.

I looked up, removed my earplugs, and said, "Hi. Can I help you?" I was nothing if not suave and debonair.

"You're one of the boys that disappeared years ago, aren't you?"

Nobody had brought that up for years, especially not a stranger. The look of puzzlement must have been clear.

She pointed to my head and said, "The white streak. I remember it."

"Remember it? From what?"

She smiled sheepishly and said, "I was the candy striper who opened your hospital room door when you woke up." She held her hand out and said, "Anna. Anna Kopelsky."

I smiled, accepted the proffered hand, and said, "Hi Anna. Jack. Jack Winterhaven. Nice to meet you. Again, I guess."

Our hands didn't immediately disengage as we silently smiled at one another.

"Would you like to get something to eat?" she asked.

I didn't have to give it another thought, studying and discipline be damned.

"I would."

I threw my books and notes into a backpack and off we went.

●●●

Due to family circumstances beyond her control, she didn't go directly to college after high school. Instead, she got a job and saved money so she could afford to go to school. She was still a year ahead of me, but that was enough to facilitate our meeting. Or our second meeting.

That she was already aware of my adventure as a ten-year-old made the whole thing easier for me. She asked questions about it and I answered to the best of my ability, which usually meant saying, "I have no idea," or "I wish I could remember." She asked me about Mike and Pete, although she didn't know them by name, and encouraged me to keep in touch with them, which I tried to do. Or so I told myself.

I didn't volunteer any information about my emotional reading abilities. It was still relatively early in our relationship and it was a secret in the genuine sense of the word. I always thought I'd tell her at some point. When the time was right and there was a reason for her to know. It's been forty years and I'm still waiting for the right time.

●●●

Being a year ahead of me, she got her undergraduate degree

before I did. So, we didn't get to see each other on campus as much as usual. Our solution was to have her move into my house. I continued my schooling while she worked at a local hospital in her specialty, pediatrics. She loved it.

We settled into a comfortable routine. I received my undergraduate degree in psychology and continued my schooling, pursuing my Master's degree in marriage and family therapy.

We got married while I was still in graduate school and, together, mapped out our life. Rather than trying to find a job, I would open a practice of my own. We thought the timing would be right. No children and no mortgage. While she stayed at her job, we could still afford to live while I struggled to get established. Then, we'd start a family, something she had always dreamed of doing. It's one reason she became a pediatric nurse.

Sometimes life kicks you squarely in the teeth.

For two years, we attempted to get pregnant. When that failed, we both underwent extensive testing, where we discovered she was infertile. The diagnosis was devastating. It took all my skills and a lot of time before we could fully cope. We talked about adoption, but in the end decided we could enjoy life and be happy with just the two of us.

We did, and we were.

●●●

It took years, but my practice finally became established and successful. I garnered a reputation for being able to get to the heart of the many issues facing the couples who came to see me. As one couple put it, it was as if I could just cut through the bullshit and see exactly what the emotional issues were, even when they were trying their best to hide the truth from not only me, but their partner and themselves, as well.

If they only knew.

●●●

Anna loved to travel. Much more than I. I think she decided that, since she couldn't have children, she would take full advantage of the freedom the circumstances afforded. Sometimes I think she loved the planning as much, or more, than the actual trip. Occasionally, I wasn't able to accompany her, so she joined an established tour group. She always met interesting people and had a great time. I was glad she found something she loved so much.

We were both interested in history, especially ancient history. Israel, Italy, Greece, and South America were all places with fascinating histories where one or both of us had been. A trip she was very interested in taking was to a site called Göbekli Tepe in the Southeastern Anatolia Region of Turkey. I had seen documentaries about the place and it looked fascinating. So, I agreed to accompany her on what could be a once-in-a-lifetime chance to visit this intriguing site.

As always, she dove headlong into the planning. We decided to undertake the trip on our own, rather than join an organized group. Regardless, we required an organized tour once at the site. Because she so enjoyed the planning, and I so detested it, she made all the arrangements. We would travel a little in Turkey and end the trip with the highlight, the tour of Göbekli Tepe. Because neither of us enjoyed cold weather, we planned the trip for August, Turkey's warmest month. Also, prime tourist season. We had to pick our poison, either too many people or too cold. Our choice made, we eagerly awaited the appointed time.

●●●

After spending some time in Istanbul and the surrounding area, we checked into the Grand Babil Otel in Sanliurfa, Turkey. Sanliurfa, also known as Urfa, was only about ten miles from Göbekli Tepe, so it was a natural choice for our stay. The city was founded in 303 BCE and, surprisingly to me, housed almost 600,000 people. The hotel's long history was reflected in its exterior architecture; however, its interior had been modernized to a five-star standard while preserving its historical character. Very cool.

Our day started when the tour company sent its modern air-conditioned bus to the hotel to fetch us. Göbekli Tepe, a UNESCO World Heritage Site, was a very popular destination, and the bus was full, mostly with older people who actually paid attention to the guide.

After parking, we stepped onto a long wooden boardwalk that wound its way toward a covered but open archaeological site, the smell of sun-warmed wood and earth rising around us. I could almost feel the buzz of expectation from the other tourists. I'll admit that I shared their sense of excitement. Being an estimated 12,000 years old, this was the oldest such site we'd ever visited, by many, many years, and, from what I'd heard, held many wonders.

We entered the covered site and stood on a raised walkway that encircled the excavation. Having done her research, Anna had packed a small pair of binoculars, which really helped.

The site contained many partial walls and partitions. The most striking figures were the many "T-stones" that dotted the area. As one might imagine, their name was derived from the distinctive "T" shape. Using the binoculars, we could clearly see the many carvings that covered the T-stones. There were both abstract and realistic carvings. Lions, boars, reptiles, snakes, foxes, and donkeys were some of the animals depicted. Strangely, there were no carvings of mythological creatures, as so many other sites contained. One of the most famous stones, the Vulture Stone, had what appeared to be three purse-like objects at the top. When I aimed the binoculars at the Vulture stone and saw these purses, a strange, tingling sensation came over me. I removed my eyes from the viewing piece and instantly felt the feeling stop. I didn't give it much more thought and continued to scan the various stones. Although there were no carvings of actual humans, some of the partial stones contained carvings that showed what appeared to be arms, hands, and a portion of a loincloth. I trained my binoculars on the hands and saw what seemed to be a bracelet, with a round, watch-like component to it, on which some figures were carved. I couldn't take my eyes from that feature, standing motionless and enthralled. The tingling feeling returned, but I was powerless to move. I stared, eyes wide open, as a bright flash exploded in my head, and I fell unconscious onto the ground.

●●●

Surprised to find myself on the ground, I awoke to an icy and wet sensation as someone gently splashed cold water on my face. My nurse wife was taking my pulse and looking into my eyes, clearly worried. When my pulse seemed normal and she knew I was responsive, she asked, "What happened? Are you OK?"

"I'm fine," I said as I sat up, supported by the railing.

Again she asked, "What happened?"

I gazed at her, a strange expression on my face. "I saw something."

"What?"

"I'm not certain, but it had to do with those three missing days. We need to get home."

# INTERLUDE #2

For some beings, boredom led them to expand their technical capabilities. These new capabilities led to breakthroughs that allowed them to explore not only their universe, but universes in other dimensions. As they did so, they encountered other beings, some less advanced and others more so. From the more advanced, they learned what they could, importing the new knowledge to their home world. But something new had happened: they had developed egos where before there were none. As their egos grew, they hoarded the new knowledge and capabilities, creating a class system that led to subservience, inequality, and strife. Inevitably, this resulted in another new phenomenon.

Violence.

With their newfound egos, some beings spent time on other, less developed worlds. There, they could mold the inhabitants as they chose, experimenting as they saw fit. Different factions sometimes chose different worlds, while at other times they elected to share a world. Some of these factions came to the dimension and universe in which Earth was located. There, they found primitive peoples struggling to stay alive. The beings, sensing an opportunity, seized it and presented themselves as they chose to be seen.

As Gods.

Some descended from the skies in elaborately decorated advanced flying machines, hoping to make a visual impression on the earthbound populace. Others, using portal technology, seemed to materialize out of thin air. Their godlike status quickly became established in each case.

They had the ability to choose different bipedal physical forms and usually chose a form meant to be awe-inspiring. Most of the time, these forms took the head of some animal and the body of an extremely large humanoid. Their colorful costumes, doused with the same pheromones they liberally spread into the environment, were designed to gently force their subjects into obedience. In return for obedience, the world was gifted with technology and an understanding of science and agriculture.

Civilization.

The structure of this civilization was based on what they had created on their home world. This again led to a class system, subservience, inequality, and strife. Of course, there could be only one outcome.

Violence.

The advanced beings had failed to overcome the patterns of their prior existence. Egos and jealousy between the factions that had settled on Earth reared their ugly heads. The worldwide War of the Gods had a calamitous effect on the planet, plunging the land into an Ice Age lasting more than one hundred thousand years. After essentially destroying the world, the beings who had survived the War of the Gods fled to their own dimension and worlds, leaving the surviving inhabitants of Earth as they had found them: struggling to survive.

# PART THREE

# AWAKENINGS

# CHAPTER 18
# SIGHTSEEING

Although I had been eager to return home, our plane tickets kept us in Turkey for two more days. After Anna confirmed I wasn't about to pass out or drop dead, she gave the green light to start sightseeing in Istanbul. Figuring we might never return, I went along, doing my best to bury what had just happened in the deepest recesses of my mind. Much easier said than done. We visited the typical tourist sites: the Hagia Sophia, Hippodrome Square, and Topkapi Palace, among them. I tried to concentrate on the wonders that stood before me, but my mind could not help but try to conjure the images of what I'd seen when I had passed out. It was like being in two places at once, with neither really able to hold my attention.

On the second day, we visited the Museum of the Ancient Orient, an almost one hundred year old institution housed in a building designed in 1883. A beautiful structure, inside and out. Maybe it was being another day removed from the passing-out incident, but I was better able to concentrate on the displays and engage in conversation. Strolling through the galleries, we were having a lovely time taking in the history that surrounded us. One of those pieces of history was an ancient Sumerian stele of Shamsh-res-usur, a former governor in the area, praying in front of the Gods. On the wrist of each of the Gods was what appeared to be a watch, or watch-like adornment. The wrist ornamentation caught my eye, and a tingling sensation immediately shot from my toes to the top of my head and down my spine. I reached out to Anna to steady myself. She took one look at me and ushered me to a stone bench about ten yards away, heavily depositing me before I could pass out. A bottle of water materialized from her bag and she thrust it into my hand.

"Drink."

I followed her instructions. As the cool liquid ran down my throat, I felt myself coming back to "normal." After drinking my fill, I pointed to the stele and said, "Would you take a picture of that, please?"

Without asking questions, she complied and quickly came back to my side. As she held her phone out to me so I could view the picture, I turned my head away and shot my arm out as if warding off an evil spirit on Halloween.

"I don't want to chance looking at it here. I'll wait until we get home."

She nodded, put the phone away, and asked, "Was it the same thing as at Göbekli Tepe?"

"It sure felt like it," I said. "And I think it was whatever those figures have on their wrists that triggered it."

Turning her gaze back to the stele, she said, "I guess we have a starting point for our research, don't we?"

I lay my head on her shoulder and said, "I think we do."

# CHAPTER 19
# CONNECTIONS

It's just like life, isn't it? I had finally made peace with the fact that I'd never know anything about what happened to me during those three days. I was happy and content in my ignorance, a state of mind for which most of us strive. Then I just had to go to Göbekli Tepe. In an instant, the experience shattered my blissful ignorance, replacing it with a longing for information. A need to know. An obsession.

Damn it!

● ● ●

Unlike when I was ten-years-old, the tools of investigation were at my fingertips. No need to ride my bike to the local library branch. A part of me wished that going to the library was still required. If it were, it would offer some respite from the need to feed my obsession at every opportunity.

● ● ●

Left to my own devices while Anna was out with some friends, I sat in front of my computer, search engine at the ready. I stared at the screen, hesitant to begin. It was as if the blinking cursor were taunting me. Daring me to begin. Although I desperately wanted to type a question, fear paralyzed me. Fear of what I might, or might not, discover.

What if it was something horrible? Something I couldn't

even begin to imagine? Or worse, what if it was nothing? No information available and I had made it all up? A hallucination brought on by years of burying in the remotest corners of my brain anything having to do with my disappearance. Was I going insane? Would I be reunited with Pete in the Asylum? An obsession paralyzed by fear is not a combination destined for success.

I stared at the flashing cursor, unable to look away. It was a metronome in my brain, but it was having the opposite effect of what a metronome was supposed to do in these circumstances. I became more agitated and nervous, unable to concentrate on the task at hand. My leg bounced, my fingers tapped, and my eye twitched. I felt as if I were about to explode.

I shoved my chair violently away from the desk, shot from the seat as if catapulted, and raced from the room.

•••

When Anna returned home, she found me sitting on the couch, staring into space. It wasn't the same couch my mother had ensconced herself in, but with a glass of single malt scotch in my hand, the scene was all too familiar. Knowing about my mother's alcoholism, she gently removed the glass, put it out of my reach on a table, and sat next to me.

"What happened?"

I stared at her, not quite comprehending the question.

Again she quietly said, "What happened?"

This time, I pulled myself together.

"I'm a complete coward," I responded.

She covered my hand with hers and said, "Tell me."

I did.

She was laser-focused on me as she listened, absorbing my words. When I had finished, she said, "I get it. It's a totally normal reaction."

As I opened my mouth to argue, she interrupted. "But," she continued, "I know you well enough to know that it's a temporary condition. In all the years I've known you, you haven't run away from anything, no matter how scary you thought it was. It's not who you are. Not even at ten-years-old."

I snapped my mouth shut before muttering, "Thank you."

"So, let it go for tonight and I'm certain you'll be ready to tackle it soon."

She kissed my forehead, stood, and, as if performing a magic trick, made the glass disappear.

●●●

I still had couples to see and a thriving practice to maintain. People who were depending on me to lead the way to marital bliss. And I still wanted to help these people in a manner which I knew only I could provide. But my wandering mind made it difficult to concentrate on the problems of others. Nevertheless, I powered through.

I thought I'd wait until the weekend, when there were no other obligations, to get "back" to my research.

●●●

The weekend rolled around well before I was ready for it, but I decided to face my fears and get something done anyway. At least that was my intention when I sat in front of my computer and began a staring contest I had no hope of winning.

"What might you be waiting for, Master Jack?"

I didn't need to turn around to know who had asked, but I did anyway.

"Sherlock. Long time no see."

In fact, it had been decades. He sat in a chair along the wall, facing me. My early iterations of Sherlock, when I was a young boy, were of the Basil Rathbone variety. Long face and nose, deerstalker hat, and Calabash pipe. Today's version was the Benedict Cumberbatch edition, dressed in modern clothing and using a smartphone. I wasn't sure which I preferred, but there was something soothing about the old version.

"Yes, indeed. A long time it has been."

"So, what can I do for you?" I asked, rather cheekily.

"Let me paraphrase one of your presidents," he answered. "Ask not what you can do for Sherlock, but rather ask what you can do for yourself."

"Oh, very subtle."

He simply nodded, his steady gaze locked onto mine. Another silent standoff—and I already knew I was going to blink first.

"Fine," I conceded. "I know I have to do this, it's just…"

He waited before saying, "It's just what, Jack?"

"It's just that I'm afraid of what I might discover," I blurted.

"Knowledge can only help, Jack."

"Yeah, sure," I pouted. "Except if that knowledge turns out to be absolutely useless. Or worse, harmful."

"Ah, I believe we have reached the crux of the matter," he said in that smarmily annoying tone. "I can assure you that knowledge cannot be harmful. At least not in this instance."

"Oh, really? And how can you make such an assurance?"

"Like this," he answered. "You have lived your entire life with no knowledge of what happened to you and your friends. And you have benefited from whatever happened, in ways you could not have imagined. However, this is not true for your companions. Pete has spent his life locked away in an asylum, being driven mad. And Mike, while he received something useful, has paid a terrible price for his gift, unable to be around people and living in lonely seclusion. Whatever knowledge you gain can only serve to help others, if not yourself."

I stared at him and then turned my gaze to the floor, ashamed.

"I see you realize I speak the truth."

I nodded, unable to utter a sound.

"And there's one more thing," he continued, a glint in his eyes.

I refocused my gaze and said, "What is it?"

"You have always suspected there was a connection between what happened to you and what happened to Ralph, haven't you?"

I thought back to that conversation with my uncle Jim all those years ago. "I have."

"The knowledge you gain may be your only hope of finding out what that connection might be."

I sat immobile, stunned by what I had heard. I nodded my thanks to him as he nodded back and his essence slowly dissipated into the universe.

# CHAPTER 20
# PURSES

With Sherlock gone, and my having learned hard truths from myself, I determined to gain the knowledge I had so longed to attain. I faced the computer screen, again having to face that never-ending blinking cursor.

"Fuck you," I said as my fingers moved over the keyboard and typed my inquiry into the waiting box. Somehow, that simple statement cleared my head and allowed me to continue.

I started simply, searching for "Göbekli Tepe carvings." Most prominently displayed on my screen was a picture of the stele which contained the three "purses." The article that accompanied the search results spoke of the supposed history of the site, as well as the possible meanings of the various carvings, all as told by professional conjecturists known as archeologists. I was not interested in the unproven opinion of others, so ignored the suppositions and concentrated on the picture.

As I continued to gaze at the picture, I could feel a stirring in my mind, which then caused my body to vibrate from within. The vibrations began at a low frequency, gradually rising before settling into a steady hum that pulsed through my skull. I held my composure, finding the sensation—not exactly pleasant, but not entirely unpleasant either. I focused my gaze on the part of the picture showing the purses, trying not to blink. The hum continued and I could feel a slight change in the vibration when…my phone rang.

Instantly, the humming and vibrations ceased, my concentration was shattered, and my frustration level was off the charts.

"Damn it!"

I checked my phone, which had continued to chirp, and saw Anna's name boldly displayed. Taking a deep, calming breath, I answered.

"Hey, babe. What's up?"

"I'm almost home. Can you meet me at the garage and give me a hand, please?"

"Sure," I said. "I'll be right down."

"Great! And don't forget, it's time to go."

Confused, I said, "Go where?"

"Really?" she said. "We're meeting the…"

Before she finished her statement, the calendar function of my phone lent a late hand. I glanced at it and finished her sentence. "Sheffield's."

"Yes. Today's the day."

I heard the garage door open, sighed to myself, and said, "On my way," as I disconnected the call and headed out.

●●●

The next day, I made my way back to the computer. Hoping yesterday's moment wasn't lost forever, I silenced my phone and repeated my search steps. Soon, I was again peering at the stele of the three "purses." Although it freaked me out a little, I was relieved when the stirring in my mind returned and my body vibrated from within. The same low frequency with a slow, steady increase in rate. It leveled off to a low, steady hum reverberating in my skull. I kept my gaze focused on the portion of the picture in which the "purses" were displayed. After what seemed an eternity, a sharp crack, like Indiana Jones wielding his whip, suddenly replaced the low hum. Instantly, I slammed my eyes shut, and a picture seared itself into my brain's visual cortex. All sound had been banished as my eyes remained tightly closed, the better to view the image which was being cast onto the back of my eyelids as if from a movie theater projector.

A single purse, not carved into stone, but three-dimensional and sitting on a surface. Maybe a floor, but made from nothing I remember having seen before. Whatever that surface was, it shimmered and changed from purple to blue to orange, all while forming swirling, interwoven patterns. The purse itself seemed to be made of a metallic material, although it had folds and creases, as if it were more of a bag than a hard metal container. The handles lay at its side, waiting for someone to grasp them and carry it away. From its interior, a faint glow barely escaped the boundaries of the object, the colors of the glow matching those of the floor's surface.

134

An unseen force thrust my eyes open, and the image before me vanished. But not from my mind. I didn't think the image would ever be erased from my mind.

I shut down the computer and sat staring at the ceiling. What had I just seen?

# CHAPTER 21
# RECOLLECTIONS?

"Your reaction to seeing the picture of those purses is troublesome," said my nurse wife.

"Well, if I'm being honest, it kind of freaked me out," I replied. "But there doesn't seem to be any residual effects," I pointed out.

"True," she reluctantly agreed. "But it's still not something normal."

"Define normal," I said, a little too snidely.

"Normal," she said in a tone meant to brook no argument, "is not having your body vibrate or your head thrumming and then exploding, and not having moving pictures burned onto the back of your eyelids."

"Well," I replied in an effort to lighten the mood, "if you're going to get technical about it, sure."

Her eye-roll was almost audible.

"But," I continued, unfazed, "it might be normal for somebody who disappeared for three days when he was ten-years-old."

That got her attention in a new way.

"Explain," was all she said.

"What if," I said, kind of making it up as I went, "that moving picture was something I was *recalling*?"

Now that I'd said it out loud, it actually made sense. I felt a surge of excitement and sat up a little straighter, trying to hide the grin forming on my face. I turned my attention back to Anna.

"Somehow, that feels right. Actually, it's the only thing that makes sense about it. Otherwise, why would I have seen it? I mean, where else could that image have come from?"

We sat in silence as we contemplated the repercussions of what I'd just said.

Reluctantly, she said, "I hate to admit it, but it does make a certain kind of sense."

I nodded in satisfaction.

"You don't recall ever having seen those purse things before? Anywhere?"

I shook my head and said, "Not that I can remember. The first time was at Göbekli Tepe, and I had a reaction there, too."

"Yes, you did." She paused for a moment, thinking. "And it wasn't just at Göbekli Tepe. Don't forget about what happened at the Ancient Orient Museum."

I mentally smacked my forehead like an old slapstick comedian. "That's right!" I thought back to the museum incident. "I was so focused on the purses that I forgot about it. And that had nothing to do with the purse things. That was some kind of bracelet."

Anna reached for her phone as she said, "And you had me take a picture."

As she searched through her phone's gallery, I felt myself becoming uneasy. I realized I wasn't mentally prepared to view that picture, or any others of that same object, without having done some research. She continued to scan through her vacation photos as I said, "I don't think I want to see that picture yet."

She looked at me questioningly.

"I remember my reaction at the museum. Before I can get into that, I need to do some research. I'm just not ready for it."

She put the phone down and said, "OK. Let's leave this for another time."

Grateful not to have to explain any further, I said, "Thank you."

"Of course," she replied, standing up. "Now, you can buy me dinner."

# CHAPTER 22
# MAKING A CHOICE

I knew what I needed to do, but couldn't bring myself to start the research into the bracelets until I had ruminated over the movie of the purse, which played on a loop in my brain. It was an image I just couldn't escape.

Had I really seen it, or was it just in my head? It felt too vivid to be random, too sharp to be something I'd imagined without a reason. I didn't have any frame of reference from which to conjure such an image. Aside from purses I'd seen being carried by people, I had never seen anything like the stone carving's depiction. Could that be it? Had I extrapolated the image based on what I'd seen Anna and others use? Could my imagination have been working overtime in what had been the unused nooks and crannies of my mind?

I suppose that could have been the case. But what about the swirling colors on the floor? Were those science fiction stories I'd been so enthralled with as a kid influencing me and my previously unknown imagination? Again, I supposed it was possible. After all, the mind, and its many recesses, was a vastly complicated mechanism. One in which even those trained in its study have very little understanding.

I was forced to conclude that, as simplistic as it may seem, anything was possible. Which, for my immediate purpose, wasn't much help.

So, I had a decision to make. If what I had seen was simply the manifestation of my imagination, impelled by the stress I was feeling over my reactions, my quest was at a standstill before it had actually begun. If, however, the image of the purse and the whirling colors was a *recollection*, and not my imagination, continuing my research may very well result in discovery.

The choice was an easy one.

●●●

I began my search as generally as possible. "Göbekli Tepe purses." To my surprise, the results were actually related to my search.

The "handbags," as most of the literature referred to them, at Göbekli Tepe, were, according to the authorities, among the oldest known to exist. While the purpose of the structures at the site was still unknown, most opinions were that it was a temple or other religious site. These same authorities had put forth the theory that the handbags were a representation of the greater cosmos. They suggested that the bag's handles, which formed a semi-circle when held upright, represented the hemisphere of the sky, while the square base represented the earth. Personally, I didn't see it, but I was certainly no expert.

What I saw, and what even those same experts should not rightly have ignored, was that images of the handbag had been carved, painted, and embroidered throughout antiquity. Everywhere. From Africa to India to China. The Assyrians of ancient Iraq and the Olmecs of Mesoamerica. The Māori of New Zealand. Literally, throughout the world. All shared the same imagery, with little or no variation. All by cultures and civilizations that had no known method of contact.

Something was happening. Something real. Yet the so-called experts turned a blind eye, ignoring evidence that was impossible to deny.

If it were true that the image I had seen was a recollection, there had to be a common thread between those ancient civilizations because they, too, had seen the same thing. Not a representation of the cosmos, of which they could not possibly have had a clue, but of an actual *thing*. An object with which they had come in contact. Something to be used, or that was being used. Something with a purpose.

Even setting aside my personal interest, this was getting interesting.

●●●

That evening at dinner, I recounted the day's search results to Anna. In doing so, I told her about the widely accepted theories and why I disagreed with them.

"So, what do you think they are?" she asked.

"I don't know," I said. "But there's no way in hell they represent the cosmos. These were civilizations that did not understand the cosmos or their place in the universe. Or the

141

concept of a universe, for that matter."

"I can't argue with that," she said. "So, where did the archaeologists come up with their theories?"

"It sounds to me that, at an archeologist's retreat, they were sitting around a campfire smoking a few doobies and someone said, 'Hey, man. I've got it. You know those handles? They look like the sky. Yeah, man. That's it. They represent the sky.'"

She laughed as she said, "And the others, after taking another hit, said, 'Oh man, that's so heavy. That's gotta be it.' And from that, a theory was born."

We laughed and continued to enjoy our dinner before engaging in our evening walk. We held hands and enjoyed the relative solitude as we strolled through the neighborhood.

"The fact that all of those civilizations had the same imagery is fascinating," Anna noted.

"It is," I agreed. "And there's no way they each came up with it independently at around the same time. There's got to be a connection."

As we continued our walk in silence, each contemplating a possible connection, I was about to say something when the scenery before me blurred out of existence, replaced by a vast, barren, rocky landscape. I stumbled over what I perceived to be a rock in my path, and Anna grasped my hand tighter, helping me to maintain an upright position. I stopped and stared at the purple-hued sky before me, unable to move.

"What's wrong?"

My head slowly moved from side to side of its own volition as I continued to stare, my mouth slack-jawed.

"Jack?"

I could feel her anxiety rising as I squeezed her hand in what I hoped was a calming gesture. I willed myself to speak, but found I could only grunt. The view before me moved forward towards some kind of structure, but my feet remained stationary. There was a hand reaching forward, holding something I couldn't see. It wasn't my hand, and I didn't know what it held because my eyes were locked on an opening in the structure ahead. The scene rushed forward through the opening, and then, as quickly as it began, it all blurred. I was back, looking at the quiet, familiar streets of my neighborhood.

I didn't need to have heightened emotional perception to feel the worry that came off Anna in waves. I looked at her and again squeezed her hand. As she saw my face and realized I was back, I could feel her anxiety level wane.

"Jack, what happened?"

"I have no fucking clue. One second I was walking with you down this street, and then I was standing in some rocky desert with a purple sky."

"What?"

"Exactly."

Ever the pragmatist, she said, "Did you see anything else? Did anything happen?"

"It did," I said, and told her everything I recalled as we continued to stand, unmoving.

The worry had returned to her as she said, "Let's go back home."

Obviously distraught, I said, "Yeah, let's."

●●●

I may have been a psychology major in college oh so long ago, but nothing could have prepared me for the fully awake, open eyes hallucination of epic proportions I had experienced. My emotions were filled with the countless negative possibilities. Scared, confused, anxious, and angry led the list. And that's without addressing the medical and mental health concerns.

The nurse in my life brought up her list of visual hallucination causes: brain damage, dementia, Parkinson's disease, delirium, schizophrenia, psychotic depression, bipolar disorder, PTSD, and diabetes, to name a few.

As we reviewed the possibilities, we confidently discounted all medical and mental health options. So, what did that leave us with?

That was an excellent question.

# CHAPTER 23
# WHAT'S REAL?

During a restless night, I couldn't help but dwell on what it was I had experienced. With that in mind, I checked on the definition of a hallucination. This from the Cleveland Clinic:

*A hallucination is a false perception of objects or events involving your senses: sight, sound, smell, touch, and taste. Hallucinations seem real, but they're not. Chemical reactions and/or abnormalities in your brain cause hallucinations. Hallucinations are typically a symptom of a psychosis-related disorder, particularly schizophrenia, but they can also result from substance use, neurological conditions, and some temporary situations. A person may experience a hallucination with or without the insight that what they're experiencing isn't real. When a person thinks their hallucination is real, it's considered a psychotic symptom.*

This aligned well with what Anna had come up with, but I still didn't think any of the known causes fit my case. Is this what Pete felt as his mother and doctors arrived at his diagnosis? He "knew," as well as anybody could, that what he was hearing was "real" and not a false perception. What is "real" anyway? How is that interpretation to be made, and by whom? Just because nobody else could hear what Pete heard, did that make it any less "real?" Did the fact that Mike could "feel" evil, and nobody else could, make what Mike felt any less "real?" And what about my ability to "feel" the emotions of others? Others couldn't feel my emotions. Did that make my ability less "real?"

For the first time, I felt real, true empathy with Pete and what he'd gone through. It made me feel like shit.

•••

"So," I said to Anna, "what do you think makes something real?"

"What!?! Where did that come from?"

"I looked up the definition of hallucination," I responded before reading the information from the Cleveland Clinic to her.

"Wow. That's a deep question," she said, stalling for time.

"It is, but let's narrow it down to 'what makes an experience real?'"

I could see her thinking, and also feel a minor annoyance coming from her. The more she thought about it, the less annoyed she became.

"You know, that's a really good question," she said. "On the one hand, if multiple people have the same experience at the same time, I suppose that would qualify as real."

"Okay," I said, "but what about the other hand?"

"Let's do what you did with 'hallucination' and ask the internet."

"OK, let's."

She got her laptop, typed in the query, and instantly received multiple answers.

Generative AI had the following to say:

*An experience is considered real when it occurs in the physical world, engaging your senses directly, and is not solely imagined or constructed within your mind; essentially, it involves a genuine interaction with your surroundings, producing tangible effects and memories that can be verified against external reality. Key aspects of a real experience: Sensory engagement: Actively perceiving the world through sight, sound, touch, taste, and smell. Physical presence: Being physically located in a specific place and interacting with objects within that environment. Emotional impact: Experiencing genuine emotions that arise naturally from the situation. Context and familiarity: The context in which an experience occurs and how familiar you are with it can influence how real it feels. Memory and recall: How vividly you can recall an experience and whether it aligns with other memories can affect its perceived reality. Subjective interpretation: Each individual's unique perspective and interpretation of an event can influence how real it feels to them.*

"Did you find that helpful?" I asked.

She reread the results and thought about them. "Not overly," she admitted.

"Yeah, I didn't think so, either. It seemed as if it basically says 'if you think it's real, it just might be.'"

"I'm not sure I get that from it," she said.

"OK, fair enough. Let's look at what happened to me through the lens of this definition," I suggested.

"Good idea."

"OK. I was in the physical world when it occurred, although I'm not sure that's what it means. What I was seeing was definitely in a physical world of some sort."

"Go on," she urged.

"My senses were definitely engaged. I tripped over a rock I didn't see, even though, physically, it wasn't in front of me. Whether it was solely imagined remains the question."

"Agreed."

"OK. Was there a genuine interaction with the surroundings? Even though my feet didn't move, the landscape did, as if I were moving within it. Also, tripping over that rock could be an interaction with the surroundings. Were there tangible effects? I definitely got closer to that structure. Does that count, do you think?"

"I don't know. I suppose it could. It was certainly tangible to you."

"What about memories that can be verified against external reality? I'm not sure I understand that statement. I can remember it, that's for sure. Verified against external reality? Not possible, at least in this instance."

"So where does that leave us?" she asked.

"Back at square one. What about that last statement? 'Each individual's unique perspective and interpretation of an event can influence how real it feels to them.' That sure seems to say that, if it feels real to you, then it's real."

"OK, now I see where you got that," she admitted. "So, if it was real to you, it must have been real."

I shrugged and said, "I guess so."

"OK," she said. "Let's assume it was real. Now what?"

"I have no idea," I responded. "Except for one thing."

"What's that?"

"Don't tell anybody else about it. I don't want to end up like Pete."

Understanding dawned. "You think the voices Pete heard were real."

"I do. And I think it was directly related to whatever happened to us."

"Ah. And you think whatever happened to you *then* is also responsible for what's happening to you *now*?"

"I do. It may be fifty years later, but I'm telling you it's all related."

"Well, shit. Now what?"

"I think I need to continue my research. This was all based on my having checked on those handbags. It's time to look into that bracelet."

"I'd tell you to be careful, but I know there's no way to do both. Be careful, anyway."

# CHAPTER 24
# BRACELETS

Purses and bracelets. Bracelets and purses. It was like I was a fashionista for antiquity.

Life is so strange.

•••

Once again, I thought I'd keep my search simple. "Göbekli Tepe bracelets." This time, the results were not as straightforward as the last. There was someone selling bronze replicas of a bracelet that didn't resemble what I'd seen. Somebody was selling a model of the site at Göbekli Tepe. There was a story about the carvings possibly being the oldest calendar in the world. Nothing relating to the bracelet.

I tried another search. "Carvings of ancient bracelets." Again, the vast majority of responses were unrelated. However, there was one response that showed promise: "Apkallu-figure Wearing Fancy Bracelets." The reference to "Apkallu" meant nothing to me. However, a picture of a carving housed at the Brooklyn Museum accompanied the headline, and this caught my attention. It was a man, very tall, with a long, square beard. He wore an impressive pair of large wings. His right arm bent at the elbow, with his hand raised and fingers relaxed, drawing attention to the bracelet around his wrist. His left arm extended forward at an angle, as though presenting or balancing something. And indeed, he was—he held a handbag just in front of him.

I couldn't believe what I was looking at! One carving with both the bracelet and purse. It couldn't have been a coincidence. Somehow, I knew they had to be related.

The article that accompanied the image identified the carving as being Assyrian. I quickly typed a new query: "Assyrian bracelets."

Mostly, I was inundated with advertisements for people selling copies of the bracelet. However, the second most abundant results were images of the bracelets, as they appeared on various carvings throughout the world. In each carving, regardless of where it had been located, be it Asia or Mesopotamia, the image was nearly identical. A round object fastened to a band that met in the middle of the wrist. The round object contained a rosette of some sort, the wide end being at the exterior rim, while the narrow tapered end met at a circle in the middle of the medallion. It reminded me of a flower.

Continuing my research into the meaning of the image, I found many differing opinions: A rosette, which symbolized good luck and protection; the Flower of Life, which was a symbol of divinity; a chamomile flower design, which the Assyrians regarded as a gift from the earth; and simply a bracelet for nothing more than decorative purposes. There was also a reference to the Anunnaki, with whom I was not familiar. There was reference to both an "Anunnaki bracelet" and an "Anunnaki watch."

I continued my search, homing in on the Anunnaki aspect of the bracelet. As expected, the opinions of the "experts" were wide-ranging. Wristbands that served as status symbols or had religious significance; a personal biofield generator; and an actual timekeeping device.

As usual, nobody, regardless of their level of expertise, had a clue.

As I reviewed pictures of various carvings, the great majority of which showed both the bracelet and the handbag, my body vibrated from within, my vision blurred, and the screen before me vanished, replaced by a room of some sort, the dimensions of which I could not determine. A pale green light bathed the room. I forced myself to turn my head to the right and found that my view also changed. The walls of the room shimmered as the color of the walls themselves changed from purple to blue to orange. On a table, set into a cradle of some sort, was a "handbag."

I felt an emotion coming from somewhere. Confusion. Although I shared the feeling, the emotion was not mine. My gaze involuntarily shifted left, revealing a wrist adorned with a bracelet. The rosette's petals, made of different colored glass or another clear material, were raised. Some blinked, some remained steady. A right hand came into view, its fingers pressing the bracelet's petals with the focused rhythm of someone working an old electronic calculator. I felt the emotional current shift—from confusion to fear—

then, just before a final petal was pressed, a quiet wave of relief. And then, suddenly, I was back, staring at my computer screen as if nothing had happened.

●●●

"Oh, my God! Are you OK?"

The worry filled her entire being before changing to full assistance mode. She profoundly needed to help others, which explains her having gone into nursing. I didn't care to be fussed over, so gently protested.

"I'm fine," I insisted. "There were no lasting effects, just as there were none from our walk."

"That may be," she said, "but something is definitely going on. Those episodes were not normal." Before I could interject, she said, "And don't start with that 'what's normal' crap. There is no universe in which what happened to you, *twice*, is normal."

I couldn't really argue the point, so didn't.

We sat in uncomfortable silence, both deep in thought. She was both upset and concerned, and I couldn't think of anything to say or do to ease either of those feelings.

Finally, Anna broke the silence. "Do you still think this has something to do with your disappearance?"

Without hesitation, I replied, "Yes, I do."

"Why?"

"Because I'm convinced that what I saw that first time was a recollection of something I'd seen. And I could only have seen something so extraordinary, and then forgotten it, during those missing three days when I forgot everything."

"So why now?" she asked.

"I don't know. Maybe enough time has passed that whatever caused me to forget is wearing off. Maybe seeing the carvings triggered a memory. Maybe it's a combination of both. Who knows? I just know, *somehow*, that it's true."

She said nothing for what seemed too long. When she looked at me and spoke, I could feel that something had changed.

"OK, you said this felt true. You also said the same thing about Pete's hearing of voices. What makes you so sure Pete was actually hearing them and not imagining it?"

I gazed at her, weighing that long-ago agreement not to tell anybody against being honest with my wife.

"Because," I quietly said, "we tested it out."

"How?"

I studied my shoes as I struggled with my dilemma. Resigned, I took a deep breath and continued.

"To tell you, I'm going to break an agreement that's been in place since I was ten-years-old. I'm going to hope that you understand and trust that you'll abide by the agreement and not tell anybody else what you're about to hear."

Gently, she said, "Of course, Jack. I only want to help."

"OK," I said. "Shortly after our release from the hospital, we revisited the place where we'd been found. It was then we'd discovered that we each had new 'abilities,' I guess you'd call them."

●●●

I spoke, uninterrupted, for more than an hour. When I had concluded my story, we sat in eerie silence. I could feel a jumble of emotions coming from Anna. I remained quiet until she had gathered her thoughts.

"Wow."

I simply nodded.

"So Pete really heard voices?"

"He did."

"And Mike. What must that have been like? No wonder he lives alone in the middle of nowhere."

Finally, she got to me.

"And you. All these years, you never mentioned it. You can actually *feel* the emotions others feel?"

"I can. It took years to get control over it, and I'm still sometimes taken by surprise, but yes. It's what makes me so good at my job."

"You could have told me," she said, hurt.

"I know. And I wanted to. Meant to. I was always waiting for the right circumstances while worried about betraying my friends. I'm sorry. That's why I said I hoped you'd understand. I know you're hurt, but just know that was never my intention."

"You're doing it now, aren't you?"

I nodded assent.

"I'm going to need some time to process this," she said. She stood, grabbed a sweater, and headed for the door. "I'm going for a walk."

● ● ●

It seemed she could have walked to Milwaukee in the time she was gone. While I waited, I forced myself to remain calm and reached out mentally in an attempt to locate her emotions, but she must have been out of range, whatever the range might have been.

My thoughts immediately went to the dark side.

*Well shit! That's a great way to fuck up a marriage. I am a complete and total idiot. I knew I should have told her years ago. Damn it!*

Not a healthy frame of mind. I couldn't really blame her for being angry, yet I held out hope that she'd find a way to forgive me. I knew in my heart she was a better person than I.

All I could do was wait.

● ● ●

And wait, I did. For almost two hours. And I was getting worried.

●●●

Anna came in, and right away, I could tell—she wasn't in a good mood. I held my tongue and waited. She moved around quietly, then finally sat next to me.

"OK, Jack, here's the deal. As you no doubt can tell, even without your special ability, I'm still pissed."

I nodded in acknowledgement.

"However, given everything that happened to Pete, and your agreement with him and Mike, I can understand your reluctance."

I let myself relax. She held one finger up and continued.

"But, if there's anything else of any kind of importance, you better tell me, and I mean now, because this is your one and only get out of jail free card."

I put my right hand over my heart and said, "There's nothing. I swear."

She stared at me hard for five heartbeats. "OK. I'll try to forget this ever happened."

Humbled, I said, "Thank you."

She nodded, rose, and said, "I'm going to bed."

As she left the room, I wisely remained seated.

# CHAPTER 25
# ACCIDENTS WILL HAPPEN

As soon as I saw Anna, I said, "Why am I here?"

*Here* was a hospital bed. Anna sat in a chair pulled up to the bedside.

"Oh, thank God!" was her response. She searched my face for a hint of recollection. When she saw only bewilderment, she asked, "You don't remember anything that happened?"

I rifled through my memory banks and shook my head. As I did, a bolt of pain shot down from my neck and traveled down my side, which caused me to wince involuntarily. I raised my hand and touched my head, feeling the bandage. Anna reached out and took my hand.

"Don't move your head too much. You have a concussion. Whiplash, too."

"Whiplash? A concussion? Was I in a car accident?"

"You were," she answered. "What can you remember?"

I took deep, relaxing breaths, trying to remember.

"Let's see," I started. "I was working on a faucet leak and needed a part, so I told you I was running out to the hardware store. I got in the car and…then I was here."

"That's it?"

"Yes," I said, trying not to get too annoyed at the question's repetition. "Did I hit someone?"

"No," she said. "It was a one-car accident. You were on a street that was not on the way to the hardware store. Someone saw your car down a small embankment, wrapped around a tree."

"Holy shit." More to myself than anything, I said, "What the fuck happened?"

"That," she said, "is the million-dollar question."

As she was about to respond, the room door opened, and a doctor entered. He approached my bed and said, "Ah, you're awake. How are you feeling?"

"My head and neck hurt, but otherwise I suppose I'm OK."

Having reached the bed, he addressed Anna.

"Hi Anna. How's the patient?"

"Hey Steve. I think he's a little shaken up and confused, but there doesn't seem to be any other damage. We've been conversing normally."

He lifted my eyelids, and pain exploded in my skull as a light like three suns scorched my pupils. "Good to know," he said casually. Then, turning to me, he added, "I'd like to keep you overnight. Just for observation."

I was about to protest when Anna squeezed my hand and said, "I think that's a good idea."

I could take a hint. "Yeah," I said. "That's probably a good idea."

He nodded and left the room as Anna said, "Who says you can't teach an old dog new tricks?"

●●●

It seemed early, but Anna had gone home, and the nurse gave me something to help with sleep. I didn't argue, thinking it would help my mind find the "off" switch. Before I knew it, I was unaware of my surroundings.

●●●

I felt relaxed as I looked at a shimmering wall. The wall was flat and glistened like blue glitter in the sunlight. No confusion. No angst. I felt as though I had become disembodied. Time was of no consequence. As the walls changed colors from blue to green to purple, I sensed a hunger rise. A hunger like I'd not felt before. It wasn't a hunger in my belly. Rather, it was a hunger that overtook my very being. I felt energy course through my body where there should have been blood. I watched as the walls turned a glittering purple hue, almost translucent. My gaze shifted to the floor, and I saw a body materialize where before there had been none. A body unlike any I'd ever seen before.

It was humanoid, but not human. The head was enormous, with four multi-faceted eyes, like a bee. Thin lips formed a mouth where I expected a mouth to be located. It had one long arm and, where the hand should have been, was a large claw, like a fiddler crab. The claw was snapping open and closed with such speed as to be a blur. Each time the claw snapped shut, a thunderous booming sound enveloped me. The other arm was short, with three very sharp-looking protrusions at the end. The being lay writhing on the floor, confusion emanating from its very core.

As I watched, the hunger within grew to where it became unbearable. I saw a hand reach for flashing lights on my wrist, changing the color of the floor and causing the body to stiffen. I moved toward the being on the floor at a dizzying speed, hands reached out to hold it, and a mouth, my mouth, covered the thin lips. Instead of biting, my mouth spread the thin lips, and I inhaled deeply. As I did so, I could taste and feel energy as it filled my soul and my appetite became satiated. Returning to my previous seat, I could feel myself relax. I looked at the now-prone body with total indifference, satisfied with my conquest. A hand once again worked the colored lights of the bracelet, the floor changed colors, and the once lively humanoid methodically dematerialized, leaving no trace of its existence.

●●●

I awoke with a crystal clear memory of my dream. Clearer than any memory of any dream I'd ever had. Other than that, I didn't give it much thought. After all, it was just a dream. An odd dream, but a dream nonetheless.

●●●

My doctor knew I'd receive better, more attentive, and

personalized care at home than I could possibly get at the hospital. So, as soon as they completed the necessary tests, they sent me home.

Most of me was more than happy to be in familiar surroundings. However, there was a part of me that knew the personalized attention would also want to delve into what had happened, and why, questions to which I had no readily available answers.

My treatment consisted of rest and acetaminophen, coupled with the occasional ice pack. My headaches came and went, getting worse if I had too much screen time. As a result, I had a lot of time to think, mostly about why I had driven my car into a ditch. Try as I might, I couldn't recall anything. I had no memory of the accident or its aftermath, other than my hospital stay. Anna explained that short-term memory loss was not uncommon after a concussion. It even had a name, post-traumatic amnesia. And its own acronym: PTA. Somehow, that information served as a comfort.

So, my assistant rescheduled my work appointments, and I embarked on a forced two-week staycation, the operative part of that being the "stay."

●●●

With all that time and not much else to do, I became fixated on the things that had happened since our visit to Turkey. Visions, memories, or hallucinations. Which were they? And why now? Fifty years had passed since I had disappeared. I thought I had buried or erased all memories of the event. Doesn't the mind protect the body and its user from traumatic events? So, even if I was too young to realize it, it must have been traumatic. Had the trauma worn off? Is that something that can really happen, or does the mind just play tricks? I convinced myself that there had to be a valid reason for everything that had occurred. Otherwise, my belief in the non-existence of coincidence was shot to hell.

A realization crept in—one long overdue: What if Pete or Mike were experiencing the same thing? It suddenly felt impossible that they weren't. I couldn't be the only one. I made a mental note to check in with them the moment I regained access to my computer.

●●●

"How's the head doing?"

I was lying on the couch, eyes closed, an ice pack resting on the bandage that still enveloped my head. Opening my eyes, I saw Anna standing next to me. I reached for her hand and said, "Better."

I had requested the ice pack because of a headache. I adjusted myself on the couch to better see Anna and said, "You know, I expected to be up and about by this time."

"It's only been a week, Jack. You must have banged your head pretty hard. Give it some more time."

I snorted a laugh and said, "It's not like I have much choice in the matter."

She sat with me on the couch and said, "Still no memory of what happened?"

I shook my head, but the pain reminded me that doing so was not a good idea. "No."

She could see the look of disappointment on my face.

"It's okay," she said in her most comforting nurse tone. "It's not uncommon for people with concussions to have memory loss for two weeks or more. Hell, some people can go months or years before recovering their memories, if they ever do."

"Is that supposed to make me feel better?" I didn't mean for it to sound so obnoxious, but it did. Ever the consummate professional, she took it in stride.

"Actually, it was. You have to understand, there's a chance you won't ever remember. A slight chance. Your concussion wasn't as bad as it could have been, so I think you should give it at least another week before deciding to really get upset about it."

Mollified, I said, "Sorry. It's just frustrating. I've never done anything like that before, and to have no memory of what happened or why is getting to me."

"I know. The best thing you can do is to not think about it. It'll come to you when you least expect it." She stood and said, "I have some things to do. Get some rest and I'll check on you in a little while."

Frustrated with my situation, I closed my eyes and tried to follow her instructions.

●●●

She might as well have said, "Try not to think about the Tyrannosaurus Rex about to eat you from behind." Instead of not thinking about it, I turned and stared directly into the huge gaping maw filled with razor-sharp serrated cutting tools. How does one ignore such an overwhelming force? The only two things I could think of were to either sleep or find something else to keep me occupied.

I tried both.

●●●

I awoke from one of my many naps and suddenly remembered something I had meant to do. Ignoring the earlier admonitions of my wife practitioner, I slowly crept to my office, sat in my desk chair, and turned the computer on before I came to my senses. Exhibiting what I thought was supreme self-control, instead of engaging in any random scrolling, I immediately opened my email account and typed:

*To: Mike Plotkin*
*Subject: Any Strange Occurrences?*

*Hey Mike. I hope you're doing well. I'm embarrassed for both of us because of how long it's been since we last communicated. Anyway, I wanted to reach out and ask if you've been experiencing any strange memories, hallucinations, or visions. Yes, you read that correctly. It's a long story, and I promise to catch you up, but in the meantime, please let me know. Even if it was something minor that you thought was nothing. Thanks. I'm looking forward to hearing from you.*

*Love*

I reread the letter and, for a moment, considered deleting it. It was cryptic and possibly alarming. Still, I didn't want to get into too much detail at this stage of the telling. Before I could reconsider, my hand shot out and hit *Send*.

I considered sending a similar email to Pete, but thought it might be best if I didn't. I was fairly certain he lacked a private email account, and sending a letter mentioning hallucinations and visions to a man institutionalized for hearing voices might not serve anyone's best interests.

Before I succumbed to the overwhelming urge to engage in unauthorized web-surfing, I hit the power button and returned to my position on the couch to take another nap. The combination of a concussion and surreptitious emailing was exhausting.

# CHAPTER 26
# A CRAZY HYPOTHESIS

As the week progressed, my head hurt less, and the sensitivity to light noticeably decreased. Anna approached as I lay on the couch, fighting mind-numbing boredom. She was clearly hiding something behind her back. I pretended not to notice her attempt at deviousness as she came to a halt.

I sat up and said, "What's up?"

"This is." She held my laptop in front of her as if bestowing upon me a tablet brought down by Moses.

"Really?" I asked as I reached for it.

"Really," she said. "You're showing progress in your recovery, and I had to do something to get rid of that pathetic look you've been wearing."

I smiled. "Thank you. I do feel better, but, man, have I been bored."

"I know. Just don't overdo it."

"No problem. It'll probably make me so sleepy that I couldn't overdo it if I wanted to."

●●●

My first order of business was to move to the kitchen table and check my email for a response from Mike.

Nothing.

I felt disappointed, but not overly surprised. It had been way too long. Probably a couple of years, but I couldn't really say for certain. I couldn't even be sure I had his current email address. Nothing to do but wait.

So, I turned my attention back to what I thought I knew. Whatever had been happening to me had started when I saw the purse and bracelet. Unable to control myself, I opened the pictures I had previously seen. I also searched for any new information. More images had surfaced, yet nothing concrete—only guesswork. I studied each picture intently. Every figure was large and humanoid. A few had wings. Others bore animal heads—birds, beasts, creatures beyond easy identification. But every one of them featured that same purse or bracelet. Sometimes both. My thoughts raced, chasing meaning through the fog—until something clicked. The dream I'd had in the hospital... I remembered it.

The dream featured a bracelet with raised petals made of a clear material and colored like the blinking lights on a 1950s science fiction spaceship. And I remembered the same thing from my other "visions." The consistency convinced me more than ever that whatever I was seeing was real. I felt it in my very core.

That's when I felt a strange sensation, as if energy were coursing through my body. The hair on my arms stood upright, and my body vibrated from within. I stiffened, unable to move, my muscles painfully convulsed and constricted. A picture appeared in my mind, and I felt a barrier shatter from within.

"ANNA!!!"

"ANNA!!!"

"ANNA!!!"

●●●

She had come running. When she saw me, the first thing she did was slam my laptop shut. She then embraced me in a bear hug and held me tight until she could feel my muscles relax and I regained some control over myself. I felt the vibrations pass through me into her, but she held me until we both relaxed.

Silently, she guided me to the couch, where I sat in shock. She placed a glass into my hand, and I unthinkingly drank as I watched her do the same.

"What happened?"

I could feel her fear as I reached for her hand. "I'm OK. Thank you."

She relaxed and repeated. "What happened?"

I told her everything I had just thought, felt, and experienced.

"We need to get you to the hospital," she said. "It sounds like some kind of seizure."

As she rose, I gently pulled her back to the couch. "That's

not what it was," I said with complete confidence.

"So, what do you think it was?"

"You're going to think this is crazy, and I mean with a capital C," I said. "I saw, or remembered, what happened while I was driving to the hardware store."

"Go on."

I could feel her skepticism.

"All right, but you have to promise to keep an open mind."

Once she nodded her assent, I continued.

"You know how I felt that what happened in Turkey was a recollection?"

Again, she nodded.

"I had a dream while in the hospital. I didn't mention it because I thought it was just that, a dream. My recollection of the dream was unparalleled. I remembered every detail. Now, I don't think it was a dream at all. I think it was something I was seeing in real time. From the point of view of somebody, or something, else."

"You're right, it sounds crazy."

I relayed the entire dream experience and included every minute detail.

"So, what makes you think it was anything other than a dream?"

"Because when I remembered what happened in the car, I felt the exact same energy. Except in the car, I wasn't seeing anything from another's viewpoint. *It* was seeing it through mine."

"I'm not following," she said.

"The dream showed me something that was happening somewhere else. In the car, the situation reversed itself. It was seeing what I was seeing. And then something happened."

"What?"

"Whatever it was, it took control."

"Took control of what? Of you?"

"Yes. It was powerful. I tried to resist but couldn't. It just laughed. I could hear it in my head. It made me drive where it wanted. When it saw the embankment and the tree, it was ecstatic. Powerless to do anything else, it forced me to press the accelerator and steer directly down the embankment and into the tree."

She stared at me, mouth agape. Whatever the emotion is called when one thinks somebody else is crazy, I felt it consuming her.

"I'm not crazy," I pleaded. "I know it's weird, but it's absolutely the truth."

She recovered enough to speak. "So, you're saying that some *being*, or other *thing*, took control of your body and tried to kill you?"

"Yes."

I thought this was a case where saying less was better than more.

"OK. For the sake of discussion, let's say you're right. Why?"

"Good question," I said, hoping to seize the opportunity. "I think what I saw in the dream, and what I felt as if it were me, was the being feeding on the energy of whatever that crab-person thing was. I think that's what it meant to do to me, Mike, and Pete, fifty years ago. And for some reason, I have no idea why, it wasn't able to finish the job with us."

"Wait. You think this thing kidnapped you?"

"Yes, I do. And for some unknown reason, we now have some sort of psychic connection."

Not knowing what to do, she stood, took a couple of steps, and returned to her previous position.

"Think about it," I said. "Let's assume I'm not crazy and look at everything that's happened. In Turkey, I saw the purse and bracelet for the first time. Then, also for the first time, I had visions, or remembrances, whatever you want to call them. Then, the more I examined the purse and bracelet, and the more pictures I saw, the more I experienced the 'visions,' some of which I believe were me seeing things through its eyes. I think it was as freaked out by it as I was."

A thought occurred to me for the first time.

"You know, I don't think it can control when it happens any more than I could. I don't think it likes not being in control, so when it saw an opportunity to rid itself of me, it took it. And I don't think it was aware of me in the 'dream.'"

I felt like I was onto something.

"Or," I continued, "that it knows what I saw in that 'dream.' That's information it wouldn't normally share with one meant to be a victim, or any being not of its kind."

I felt the crazy emotion fade from her, replaced by thoughtful consideration. I let her take her time. Finally, she got there.

"So, assuming you're not crazy, and I'm still not totally convinced, let's say you've made a reasonable case for a totally outlandish hypothesis." She paused, and I remained silent. "So, now what?"

"I don't know," I replied. "But I think that, whatever has to be done, I've got to do it with Mike and Pete. It was the three of us to start with, and it's going to have to be the three of us to finish it."

"Shit," she said. I wasn't certain if she had resigned herself to the truth of what I'd said, or if she was just placating me. "This is absolutely crazy, but assuming you're right, what's next?"

# CHAPTER 27
# ANNA'S JOURNAL ENTRY #1

*God knows I've always strived to be a supportive life partner. As has Jack. For the most part, I've felt we've both done an admirable job. But these latest developments have really put me to the test.*

*I've always approached life with a scientific mindset— rational, analytical, firmly rooted in logic. So the revelations Jack has laid on me have left my mind spinning. And to make things even more complicated, knowing he can feel my emotions has made me put up walls I never imagined I'd need. My dilemma is that I want to be supportive, but if I let him feel my true emotions about what he's shared, he'll know my true feelings. And how scared I am for him.*

*He has truly come to believe that he has a psychic connection with some unknown "being" that kidnapped him when he was ten-years-old. The fact that he disappeared when he was ten is beyond dispute. But the thought that anything other than another person could have been responsible rips the fabric of reality to shreds. Add to that the fact that he thinks this being could exert physical control over him, and possibly vice versa, and I can't help but feel he has become totally delusional.*

*How far can I go with my particular brand of deception? If I push back too much, I could lose his trust. And I don't want that to happen. I want to be there for him and to help in any way I can, but I also need to protect his long-term mental well-being.*

*Shit! I hate this.*

*For now, I have to play along with his hypothesis. Be there for him, physically and mentally. It's the only chance I have to save him.*

# INTERLUDE #3

After fleeing Earth and returning to their home dimension and worlds, the beings who had dominated life on Earth for so long floundered. They were once again living full-time amongst peers and could not present themselves as gods. The other inhabitants advanced and shared technology during the beings' time on Earth, giving them a less-than-welcome reception on their return. The vast majority of their kind ostracized them, so after failing to learn how to cope with their new status, they took their bruised egos, boarded ships, and went in search of new worlds.

Some found uninhabited worlds and settled, using technology to mold their new environments to their specific needs. Except for one aspect of their home world, which they could not duplicate: the energy that sprang from the planet itself and fed life, including the beings themselves.

They set about attempting to artificially replicate the energy source. Over the next millennia, they ceaselessly experimented, never quite getting what they needed. They came close. Close enough where they could survive, but not thrive. Their version of subsistence farming.

So, they changed the focus of their research.

They knew the location of what they needed. It was just a matter of discerning how to get it without arousing the suspicions of their former planet-mates. With a renewed purpose, they worked to create a vessel. A vessel that could travel, land, and remain hidden. They repurposed existing portal technology, making it smaller and more portable. They created new materials that could withstand both the vacuum of space and the pressure of deep oceans. And finally, they were ready to test their creations.

A small party of four made the first incursion. They were the dominant force behind the research and felt they deserved the honor. Others were willing to let them take the risk.

They materialized in a remote, almost deserted area of their home world. The cube in which they traveled remained invisible. As they exited the container and their limbs touched the ground, they stopped and absorbed the pure energy they had so long sought. Motionless, they stood, gaining strength and confidence. The energy fed not only their bodies, but their spirits. And their egos.

As they re-energized themselves, another of their kind wandered into the clearing in which they stood. Instantly, they were identified as intruders. Recognizing the danger, they descended upon the lone home-worlder, engaging in the violence which their ancestors had used to wreak havoc on Earth.

During the melee, the leader of the four, driven by sheer instinct, placed its mouth over the mouth of its victim. As it inhaled deeply, the home-worlder's struggles slowly subsided, until it lay still and lifeless. The leader stood back and stared at the body, realization dawning.

It had sucked the life-energy from the being, and it felt wonderful. The result was more invigorating than it could have imagined. The power of the life-energy was concentrated, like diving into the center of the planet's energy source. And there was another thing. A totally new sensation.

It was delicious.

●●●

The four returned to their adopted planet, reinvigorated, both physically and mentally. They realized that if one being could provide so much sustenance, there was no need to replicate the energy source of the home planet. The universe teemed with life forms. Those life forms were filled with energy.

Delicious energy.

They already had the basics of the technology that would be required to travel not only in their universe, but in the infinite universes of the infinite dimensions. Some tweaking might be necessary, but they could easily address that.

A smorgasbord of energy awaited.

●●●

They worked to perfect the technology and, through its use, their methodology. Through experimentation, they discovered that different beings in different universes had different energies. Unique properties with different effects.

And unique tastes.

Like many beings, they developed an appetite for sweet things. Especially after feasting on more savory energy. As if trying various restaurants to find the most satisfying dessert, they scoured the many universes and came upon their favorite.

Earthlings between the ages of seven and twelve years old. Ten-years-old was the true sweet spot.

# PART FOUR


# REUNIONS

# CHAPTER 28
# WHAT GOOD ARE REASON
# AND LOGIC?

Three days had passed since the latest revelations, and Anna had cleared me for limited screen time. The first thing I did was check my email, where I found a response from Mike:

*Hey Jack. Sorry I couldn't get back to you sooner. I went off-grid for a couple of weeks, just to clear my head. I'm a little embarrassed about how long it's been, too. Thanks for reaching out. So, memories, hallucinations, or visions, huh? I've not experienced anything like that. I'll assume from your email that you have. And since you're asking if I have, I'll also assume that it has something to do with our disappearance. After fifty years. I'm definitely intrigued. Let's go old school and actually speak. Let me know when it might be a good time. Take care. M*

I was more relieved to have received a response than I could have imagined. It had been so long since we had communicated that I was unsure about the status of our relationship. The fact that he was willing to talk gave me hope we might pursue whatever this was together. Reading his response and what he had extrapolated from my simple question reminded me of how his mind worked. I felt confident that together, we could make significant headway.

If I could convince him.

•••

"Hi, Mike."

"Jack! It's good to hear your voice."

"And yours," I said.

We spent the next fifteen minutes catching up and generally shooting the shit. It felt good to have my friend back.

"So, what's this about memories, hallucinations, and visions?" he asked.

"Get comfortable. It's a long, complicated, and strange tale," I responded.

Then I launched into my story. I started at Göbekli Tepe, took him to the museums, explained my research and the theories I'd come up with, detailed my various experiences, told him about the car accident and what I believed was the reason behind it, relayed the details of the hospital dream and what I actually believed it to be, and explained the reasoning behind my ultimate hypothesis.

"So," I said, "am I ready to join Pete, or what?"

"Wow. That's a lot to take in," he said. "I'll be honest. Joining Pete may not be out of the question."

I strove to detect a hint of joking in his voice.

"I know, and I'm sorry to lay it all on you at one time. I'll understand if you need some time to digest it."

"Time would help. Definitely."

"Any initial impressions you could share?" I asked, trying not to plead.

"Well, you've laid out reasonable and logical reasoning to back up your hypothesis, which is impressive. The more so because the hypothesis itself is more than a little bizarre. This is way out of my wheelhouse. I'm used to dealing with psychopaths and killers."

I laughed. "Who'd have thought I would bring you something that could make them seem normal?"

"Yeah. Who'd have thought?"

"Let's do this," I suggested. "Take some time to think about what I've said. In the meantime, I'll send you copies of the pictures I saw, just so you can see that there's concrete proof of the purse and bracelet. Maybe do some research of your own. Then get back to me."

"That sounds reasonable."

"Great," I said, hoping my enthusiasm would be contagious. "I'll get those out to you today."

"Sounds good." He paused. "And Jack."

"Yeah?"

"Be careful."

●●●

"How'd it go with Mike?"

Anna and I were having dinner, and she caught me with a mouthful. I held up my index finger as I chewed and gulped.

"He thinks there's a chance Pete and I might soon be roommates."

This time, I had caught her in the middle of a swallow, and she tried not to choke.

"What?" she sputtered.

I repeated the conversation for her as accurately as I could.

"You can't really blame him for being skeptical," I said, feeling the need to defend Mike's reaction. "You thought it sounded pretty crazy at first, too."

"I'm not denying that," she replied, her tone defensive. "Especially for someone who's spent so long dealing in the black and white of police work."

"Good point."

"Did you send him the pictures?" she asked.

"I did."

"Let's see if they jog any memories for him," she said.

●●●

Two days later, I received the following email:

*To: Jack Winterhaven*

*Subject: Purses and Bracelets*

*Hey Jack. Thanks for sending those pictures. As you suggested, I did some digging on my own—and just like you said, there's nothing even close to a definitive answer about either of the objects. Based on that, and the fact I don't share your memories, hallucinations, or visions, I don't know what I can do with this. I'm sorry, but, to be honest, I'm also a little relieved. If you can think of anything specific I can help with, I'm more than happy to give it a shot. In the meantime, think about seeing a professional to help you deal with it. I wish I could offer more.*

*Love you, brother*

Well shit. If I couldn't convince him about the reality of my experiences, what hope was there with a total stranger?

I showed Anna his response, and I believe she was as disappointed as I was. I remained convinced that, if there was anything to be done, it would require all of Mike, Pete, and me to take part.

My sense of isolation was complete.

●●●

There was nothing to be done but to carry on with life. I saw clients and went through the motions of eating, reading, exercising, and all the other mundane motions of everyday living. No matter what I was doing, my mind kept circling back to my hypothesis and how close I might be to uncovering what I believed to be the truth. I once thought I'd made peace with the idea of never knowing—but now I understood that remaining in the dark would be a devastating blow to my mental well-being.

I was lost.

# CHAPTER 29
# WELCOME ABOARD

Depression was gnawing at me, so I spent the evening with Anna and a show that was pure nonsense. My brain couldn't have survived a coherent plot. Maybe "reality" TV is just mercy programming for the mentally exhausted.

To my surprise, she was also having a difficult time dealing with Mike's response. We both understood it, but, perhaps unrealistically, had expected more. Something with a positive bent.

Television no longer holding our interest, we called it a night and went to bed.

●●●

The sound of my phone scared the crap out of me and woke me from a deep sleep. It didn't do much for Anna's sleep, either. I reached for the phone and saw two things: one was that it was two o'clock in the morning, and the other was that the call was from Mike. I showed both to Anna, sat up, and answered, putting the call on speaker.

"Mike. Is everything all right?"

"No, Jack. Everything is not all right. In fact, everything is fucked. More to the point, I think you and I are going to be roommates with Pete."

I glanced at Anna. "Are you telling me you've had the memory, hallucination, and vision experience?"

"Yes! That's exactly what I'm telling you! What the fuck!?!"

I could feel his extreme agitation. Rather than talk about what had happened, I thought it might be more helpful to try to calm him.

"Mike, it's going to be OK. I know how disconcerting that can be, but I'm here to tell you that there aren't any lasting or side effects. Just breathe."

I heard him taking deep breaths and counting backwards from twenty. With each breath and recited number, I felt him grow calmer.

"Good. Just keep it up until you feel that you can talk normally."

After another round of twenty breaths, he said, "Thank you."

"No problem. Are you OK?"

"Yeah, I'm OK. But shit, that freaked me out more than any serial killer I've ever dealt with. And let me tell you, that's saying something."

"I can only imagine. Do you want to talk about what happened now or wait until you can process it a little more?"

"I think waiting and processing is a good idea."

"So do I," I agreed. "I have to work tomorrow, but I'll be free tomorrow night. Let's talk then."

"Sounds like a plan."

"Good. Try to get some sleep."

"Will do. And Jack, I'm sorry for doubting you."

"No problem. I've been doubting myself lately."

●●●

When I walked in the door after work, the first thing I heard was Anna calling to me.

"Have you heard from Mike?"

I walked into the kitchen to find her pulling a frozen pizza from the oven.

"Not yet. I told him I'd be available tonight, so it's a little early."

"I just thought he might've called early. Just in case, I made pizza. It was quick, easy, and we can eat it fast, so you're ready for his call."

I laughed. "A little eager to hear what he has to say?"

"Oh, yeah. I'm eager to know if you're going to have another roommate at the Asylum."

"Proving I'm insane?"

"Exactly!" She laughed as she said it. "Either that or he's going to back you up."

"Either way, it would be very comforting," I replied as we

prepared to devour the pie.

"All kidding aside," she said, "what do you think happened?"

I shrugged. "Who knows? The only thing I can think of is that he was researching the purse and bracelet things and, somehow, that awakened something. At least that's what I think happened to me, so it's reasonable to assume it happened to him, too."

"Sounds about right," she said

"It shouldn't be long before we know for certain."

●●●

"I'm sorry for waking you up in the middle of the night," Mike said.

"No problem. Actually, I was more than a little relieved to get the call. That alone was enough to let me know I wasn't imagining the whole thing."

"Sorry for doubting, but you can't really blame me."

"And I don't. It's an unbelievable story. I get it," I said. "Tell me what happened."

As he spoke, I interrupted.

"Before you start, do you mind if I put this on speaker? Anna's been dealing with me, and I think it will be good to have another opinion."

"No, go ahead. Hi Anna."

"Hi Mike. How are you?"

"You tell me after you've heard my story."

"Deal."

My phone was between us on the couch. We sat back and waited.

"OK. Sometimes I have trouble falling asleep. Last night was one of those times. So, I went to the computer and started scrolling. Aimlessly at first. Then I remembered the pictures you'd sent and did more research. A bunch of pictures came up. It was amazing. There were carvings from all over the world, all showing basically the same thing. Some kind of being holding a purse and wearing that bracelet, just as you'd described."

He paused, and I could tell he was considering the best way to proceed. His decision having been made, he continued.

"Then, and there's no other way to describe this, I wasn't looking at my computer monitor anymore. Instead, I was looking at what must have been walls. Shimmering walls that changed colors. Like a party in the 70s. Then my perspective changed, although I hadn't moved. I looked down at the floor, which was also changing colors. And there was some kind of…not a person, but almost like a person, lying there. It didn't move. I'd seen enough dead bodies to know one when I saw one, and this one was dead. Then the color of the floor changed, and the body…well, it

192

disappeared. Like it was on a Star Trek transporter pad. Then my perspective changed again. I was looking at some kind of pillar. It might have been stone, it might have been something else. I couldn't really tell. The pillar was an upright 'T' shape. Anyway, I saw a hand appear. It 'felt' like it was my hand, but I know that can't have been. In the hand was something that looked like a branding iron. It was round with three lines forming something that looked like a peace sign, or a modified Mercedes-Benz emblem. 'I' walked toward the pillar, and as 'I' approached, an opening appeared on the side of the pillar. It matched the three-pronged wheel of the branding iron thing. A hand, my hand, came up and inserted the end of the branding iron into the opening. The interior of the pillar shimmered. I walked into the pillar and then… then I was back in my house staring at my computer screen."

Anna broke the silence when she said, "Wow."

"Yeah," Mike agreed. "Wow. Although that wasn't the first thing I said."

"That matches up so closely with my experiences that it has to be connected," I said. "Not what actually happened, but the experience itself, and how you felt during it. Not to mention the similarities."

"Mike," Anna said, "how did you feel, physically? Any headaches or other side effects?"

"Nope. One minute I was here, then I was there, then I was back. Except for freaking me out, I was perfectly fine."

"And I have to ask," she continued, "you haven't hit your head recently, have you?"

He laughed and said, "Unfortunately, no. That would have provided a convenient excuse."

"My turn with an 'I have to ask' moment," I said. "Did you feel the presence of evil?"

He hesitated, and I jumped in. "Yes, Anna knows. About all three of us. Sorry, she's a part of this now and I had to tell her."

"Mike, I promise that your secret is safe," Anna assured him.

I could hear his intake of breath. "Yeah, I suppose you did, Jack. So, to answer your question, yes. I did. It was just like I remembered from when we were kids."

"And I could feel its emotions when I was having my experiences. Does that tell us anything?"

"Other than our abilities haven't faded, which we already knew, I don't see what," he responded.

"Me neither," I answered. "What do you think of my hypothesis that whatever we're seeing, or seeing through, was what grabbed us?"

"I think it's the only thing that makes sense about this," he said.

Silence followed as we contemplated the implications. Anna broke it when she said, "So, now what?"

"If I were working this as a case at the FBI, and knowing what I know, I'd say there was an obvious missing piece."

"Pete," I said.

"Yeah, Pete," he agreed.

"I thought about sending him the same email I sent to you," I said. "But, after considering it, didn't think it was the best idea, based on his circumstances."

"Probably a good thing you didn't," Mike said. "Let's not rush into anything, especially since we don't know what we're dealing with."

"Agreed," I said. "Let's give it a few days and see what we can come up with."

"Sounds like a plan, Jack. Bye Anna. Later."

We disconnected the call and looked at one another.

"So, what do you think?" Anna asked.

"I think I'm glad to have Mike aboard what I hope isn't a sinking ship," I responded.

# CHAPTER 30
# WE KNOW WHAT WE KNOW

"I could feel the malevolence," Mike said. "It's a good thing I was only walking my property and not driving like you were."

It was two days after we had last spoken, and Mike had called to inform me of his latest experience.

"I could feel it controlling my movements, looking for a way to harm me. I was in a pretty level area, so, except for some rocks, there was nothing to cause too much damage. Still, it found a way to make me trip over a large rock. Luckily, I avoided hitting my head. I could feel it withdraw as soon as I hit the ground."

"We can't keep living like this," I said, my frustration on full display. "We have to figure out a way to take control, or at least limit its control."

"I don't disagree, but how can we come up with a plan if we have no idea what we're dealing with?"

"I was hoping the FBI agent in you would have an answer to that question."

"OK, let's break this down by what we know, or think we know," he suggested.

"That should take us about two minutes," I replied.

He laughed. "Maybe, but I think you'll be surprised once we start to talk it out."

"Surprise me," I said.

"OK. We think we know that this being is what grabbed us. We've seen what it does to its victims. We don't know how, but we definitely know it results in death," he recounted. "You with me so far?"

"Keep going," I said.

"We know, or think we know, that it has some kind of advanced technology."

"What makes you say that?"

"The purse thing you saw in a cradle, the bracelet with what seems to be some kind of keypad control, the pillar with the three-prong key it disappeared through. That all has to be some kind of tech."

"Got it. Good points, but so what?"

"We'll see. Let's keep at it."

"Sorry," I said. "Didn't mean to be such a buzzkill."

He ignored that entirely. "So, technology—right. That means this isn't some all-powerful, god-like being."

"Which means," I contributed, "that it should be susceptible to something. Maybe a weapon."

"And," he continued, "you mentioned you believed it had no

more control over our contacts than we do, which implies it can be taken by surprise."

"Speaking of control, if it can control our actions, like driving me off a cliff and tripping you over a rock, might we assume that we could do the same to it?"

"Good point," he said. "But there's still something we're missing."

"I don't doubt it," I said. "Any ideas?"

"Maybe. There's an inconsistency, and those drive me crazy."

I could feel him deep in thought and let him work it through without interruption.

"Why didn't it finish us back when it had us? We saw what it did to those other victims. Yet we still walked away, even if we had no memories. That's more than the others can say."

"Maybe," I hesitantly said, "it was because there were three of us. In each of the incidents we saw, there was only one victim."

"That's it! That's got to be it! It's the inconsistency! Somehow, the fact that there were three of us stopped it from sucking the life from us."

"So, as we suspected, it's going to take the three of us to fight it," I said.

"I believe it will," he agreed. "See, you never know what you know until you know it.”

Laughing, I said, “Very profound, Mystic Mike.” On a more serious note, I said, “Please tell me you have a plan.”

“Not yet, but we’ll come up with something. Here’s what I think we need to figure out. We’ll need to spring Pete from the Asylum, hopefully willingly. If not, are you up for some good old-fashioned kidnapping?”

“I’d rather not, but let’s cross that bridge when we have no other choice.”

“Yeah, I’d rather not. The Bureau really frowns upon kidnappers. OK, we’ll also need to figure out where that thing will be, and when, and how to get into its lair, or whatever that place is.”

“Should be a piece of cake,” I said.

“Yeah. We have our work cut out for us, but at least we know what we know.”

“Let’s reconvene in a few days and see what we’ve come up with separately,” I suggested.

“Talk to you in a few days,” he responded, just before disconnecting.

●●●

“That all seems to make sense,” Anna said.

We were rehashing my most recent conversation with Mike.

"It does. But it still leaves the dilemma of what we're going to do and how we're going to do it."

"The way I see it," she said, "the only way you're going to find where that guy is, is with Pete and Mike."

"Why?" I asked.

"Because your ability to feel emotions won't be much help. I mean, it wasn't much help fifty years ago when you were testing out your control. At least that's what you told me."

"Well, shit," I said. "You're right, of course. They're the ones who could either hear voices or feel the evil. That's really how we knew we were in the right location. So either of them could do it without me."

I found that realization depressing, knowing that I wasn't a necessary component of the operation, and told Anna as much.

"You know, I'll bet that's how Pete felt."

"What do you mean?"

"As far as what you and Mike were able to do with your abilities. You both got careers out of what happened. All he got was locked up."

"Damn, that's insightful. And it sounds right. I never thought about it in those terms."

"Well, just keep that in mind when you go to get him."

"I will. Thank you."

"So, that still leaves the problem of how you'll know where and when to go."

"Any bright ideas?" I asked.

She thought about it, and I could almost see as the realization occurred.

"You said the being didn't seem in control of when your connections happened. What if you could figure out a way to control when it happened?"

"Then what?" I said, intrigued.

"Then you just kind of hang around without making it do anything or noticing your presence. Just kind of eavesdrop. Hear what you could hear, see what you could see."

"And see if it reveals anything?" I considered the prospect. "That might work."

"It might. It's already revealed a lot without knowing about it."

"OK, but how?"

"Hey," she said good-naturedly, "one step at a time."

# CHAPTER 31
# THAT CAN'T BE

I reconnected with Mike and told him about the "plan" Anna and I had come up with. Admittedly, it wasn't much of a plan yet. But it was the beginning of a concept for a plan.

"That makes sense, from an operational standpoint," Mike said.

"Which part?" I asked.

"The part about taking control," he said. "You know, the best defense is a good offense. I think it works in this case."

"OK," I said. "Any brilliant ideas about how we do that?"

"Actually, I think it just might be a matter of intention."

"You've already lost me, Mike."

"Suppose you or I—or maybe both, separately—do something we think has a good shot at getting us in touch with the being. Something that's caught us off guard in the past but actually did it."

"You mean like those purse or bracelet pictures?"

"Exactly. Only this time, instead of letting it happen by accident, we lean into it—mentally speaking."

"So basically, we will it into happening?"

“I guess that’s one way to characterize it.”

“Have you had much success doing this in the FBI?” I inquired.

“I can’t say that I have,” he replied. “But, unless you have another suggestion, I think we should try it.”

“Why not,” I said. “What have we got to lose?”

“Not a damn thing,” he said.

“OK, let’s give it a shot.” I realized he said something earlier that needed some clarification. “Hey, you said before that we shouldn’t both try it at the same time. Why?”

“Because if we’re trying for stealth, I thought both of us making contact at the same time might defeat the purpose.”

“And that’s why you’re the FBI agent,” I noted. “All right, I’ll send you a list of times that I might be available to try, and then we can coordinate.”

“Great. It always feels good to have a plan to take control of an investigation. Fingers crossed.”

●●●

I told Anna about the plan, and she couldn’t have been more enthusiastic.

“Let’s try it now,” she said.

“Now? Like right now?”

“Yes. Why not?”

She could see my hesitancy. "I don't know. I just thought I'd do something to prepare first."

"Like what, calisthenics? Come on, I'll pull up some pictures."

And just like that, she ran off to grab my laptop and brought it back into the living room. She opened it, did a quick search, and picture tiles filled the screen.

"Wait," I said. "Before you open any of those, let me text Mike and let him know. I don't want to screw up the plan on the first attempt."

I grabbed my phone and my fingers went to work:

"Hey Mike. I'm going to give our plan a shot now. Just let me know you're not doing the same."

I glanced at Anna as I waited for the reply. She smiled as if all was well with the world and this was how people normally spent their time.

My phone dinged to indicate a text message. It was from Mike:

I showed the response to Anna, who returned the gesture in three dimensions and handed the computer to me.

"I'll let you do the honors."

Trying to muster some enthusiasm, I said, "Great," as I

accepted the computer and chose a picture. It showed both the purse and the bracelet. I concentrated, stared at the items, and thought about being intentional.

And then I was in a room, not in our home.

●●●

"Well, that was a complete waste of time," I said as soon as I saw Anna again.

"Why do you say that?"

"Let me clarify. It wasn't a waste of time in the sense of being able to get wherever it was I went. In that sense, it was a success. It was a waste of time because I was there for literally two or three minutes and discovered absolutely nothing."

The look on her face clearly indicated that she thought I was insane.

"What are you talking about? You were there for an hour. I timed it."

"That's not possible," I said, completely confident.

"It's not only possible, it's accurate," she said, trying not to be overtaken by anger.

"How can that be?"

"Tell me what happened," she commanded.

"I got there…"

"Where is 'there'?" she interrupted.

I gave the question some thought before answering. "I'm not certain, but I think it was a dwelling of some sort. Maybe where the being lived. It definitely wasn't the same place I'd seen before."

"OK. Sorry. Go on."

"So, I got there and saw a room. It was sparsely furnished, but it had a couch and some chairs, which is what made me think it was a house. None of the materials looked familiar. It was light, but I couldn't see a light source. I concentrated on being intentionally quiet, although I had no idea how to do that. It must have worked because I didn't get the sense it had detected my presence. I watched as it turned to look at a wall. On the wall was a square object with three concentric circles of lights flashing at regular intervals, but not in unison. It reminded me of a clock, although it had no recognizable hands or numbers that I could see. As soon as the being saw this object, I could hear its thoughts. Somehow, I understood it. Maybe because I was in its head and not hearing them spoken externally. I don't know. Anyway, it basically thought, 'Damn, I need to leave in two chrons.' It moved to a piece of furniture I hadn't seen, grabbed something, and walked to the wall. A door appeared, it/I went through, and I was back here."

"That's it?"

"Yes. That's why I said it could only have been a couple of minutes. I think a 'chron' is what it calls a minute. It was definitely in a hurry, like it was late for something. So, there's no way it could have been an hour."

Wordlessly, she picked up her phone and handed it to me. The screen displayed the stopwatch function and showed 60:01.02. I stared at it, uncomprehending.

"I started the stopwatch as soon as I saw you'd made contact. And I stopped it as soon as you got back."

I was speechless and helpless to do anything but look from the stopwatch to Anna, and back again. Finally, I recovered enough of my senses to utter, "What the fuck?"

●●●

The awareness of the differing times threw us for a loop. We tossed some theories around, none of which made any actual sense. Then I realized that another point of view might be helpful.

"Let's call Mike," I suggested.

"Good idea."

●●●

"That definitely sounds crazy," was Mike's comment after listening to our story.

"Thanks for that confirmation, Agent Plotkin," I smarmily replied.

I could feel his amusement as he said, "Glad to put my expertise to good use."

"I swear, it's like you're both still ten-years-old," Anna commented.

Simultaneously, Mike and I replied, "Thank you."

All she could do was laugh.

"Seriously, at first blush it sounds crazy," Mike said. "But let's look at it logically."

"Let's," I said.

"OK. First, let's assume that you're both correct."

Anna, back in serious mode, said, "OK, although both those things don't really seem possible."

"Don't they?" he replied. "What time is it in Chicago?"

"6:00 p.m.," she responded.

"And yet, here in Montana, it's 5:00 p.m."

"That's not the same thing," Anna said. "While there are different time zones, an hour is still sixty minutes in each."

"Good point," I said, mostly so I could feel as if I was contributing.

"It is a good point," agreed Mike. "So, if time moves at a different rate wherever Jack went, what does that suggest?"

Anna and I looked at each other, baffled.

"Tell us," she encouraged.

"To me, it suggests that our not-so-friendly kidnapper isn't from around here."

"Not from around here, like the U.S.? Or not from around here like an ET?" I asked incredulously.

"More like the ET, of one sort or another," he said. "Look. A day on Earth is twenty-four hours, because that's how humans have defined it. And a year, while we calculate it to be 365 days, is one revolution around our sun, no matter how we calculate the length of a day. Right?"

We both nodded, and I responded, "So far. Go on."

"OK. A year here is 365 days. But it takes Mars 687 of our days to make one revolution around that same sun. So if we say something took a year here on Earth, and someone on Mars said something took a year there, to us it would seem as if the Mars occurrence actually took almost two years."

"Holy shit," I said. "So you're saying that when we had our experiences connecting with the kidnapper, we were actually on another world somewhere?"

"I'm saying it's a theory that matches your time-keeping experience."

"And when you say 'somewhere,'" Anna asked, "where are you talking about?"

"I have no idea," he responded. "It could be a different solar system or galaxy for all we know. Hell, it could even be another dimension."

"This is pretty fantastical," Anna said. "You've spent a lot of time watching Marvel movies, haven't you?"

"There's not a lot to do in the middle-of-nowhere, Montana. But the concept of the multiverse has been around since 1895."

"How do you know this stuff?" I asked.

"Have I mentioned that there's not a lot to do in the middle-of-nowhere, Montana?"

# CHAPTER 32
# ANNA'S JOURNAL ENTRY #2

*Jack was back in touch with his old childhood friend, Mike Plotkin. Since Mike had been an FBI agent, I figured he might bring a stabilizing influence to their investigation. He'd dealt with plenty of real-world madness before, and this situation with Jack seemed to fall neatly into that box.*

*Oh, I couldn't have been more wrong! What the fuck! How can a trained law enforcement officer, with years of experience, buy what Jack was pedaling? Not only buy it, but actively participate in its manufacture?*

*I can see where they are headed with this. It's inevitable. They are going down the alien rabbit hole.*

*Is there anything I can do to pull them out of it? I'm really worried. More worried than ever. I'm not sure there's anything I can do at this point but to let them follow this road to its inevitable, disappointing conclusion. I'll just have to be there to pick up the remaining Jack pieces.*

# CHAPTER 33
## A CREATURE OF HABIT

"Aliens? Really?"

After a night's sleep on the idea, Anna wasted no time in mentioning it again.

"I don't know," I said. "It feels pretty far-fetched."

"Far-fetched? That's the nicest thing you could call it," she replied.

"You make it sound like the whole thing offends you," I said.

"Well, now that you mention it, it does. It seems that 'aliens' is the go-to excuse whenever anybody can't figure something out. Who built the pyramids? Oh, it must have been aliens. Give me a break."

The depth of her feelings on the subject astonished me, and I told her so.

"It just seems like the easy way out," she insisted.

"There are instances when I would agree with that, although I'm definitely more open to the idea than you are. There's an awful lot in history that can't be explained."

"So, of course, it's because of aliens. I don't buy it."

"I know you don't. And just to throw gasoline on this fire, if you do research into the beings wearing the bracelets and holding those purses, there is quite a lot of speculation about them being aliens masquerading as Gods. The research points out the undeniable fact that nearly identical carvings, showing the same items, appear throughout the ancient world in all kinds of civilizations that had no known contact. How would you explain that?"

"Coincidence. Mutual simultaneous evolution. Mass consciousness. I don't know, but I'm not going with the alien theory."

"OK, I can respect that. So, what about our different time experiences? You can't deny that it happened."

"Can't I?" she said defiantly. "What I can't deny is the time kept by my stopwatch. I can, however, deny your explanation of what the time was wherever you think you were. You're operating under the assumption that your interpretation of the thing on the wall with the flashing lights was a clock and that the kidnapper was referring to a period of time when it mentioned 'chrons.' Maybe that interpretation is incorrect. Maybe it just felt like time went by quickly when, in fact, it was actually an hour. I'm not ready to take that leap of faith."

"We've been calling this a 'thing' or a 'being' the whole time—doesn't that at least hint at the possibility of 'alien'? That's one of the reasons your reaction surprised me."

"I was trying to placate you. Hoping you'd come to your senses. There are plenty of monsters of the human variety. I can view them as a 'thing' or 'being' without thinking about aliens. The thought of the kidnapper being anything other than human, at least on the species level, never occurred to me. And you've never seen anything attached to it that hasn't appeared to be human."

"What about that fiddler crab thing and the other things I've seen? And Mike, too? The rooms, the lights, the dematerialization of the bodies?"

"Have you never seen a movie or been to an amusement park? Those things aren't real or alien. People set up all kinds of fantasy or role-playing scenarios in their homes. Or dress up for Comic Con. That doesn't make them aliens. It makes them good with make-up and technology."

I knew when it was time to stop beating the proverbial dead horse. "I guess time will tell, if we ever get to the bottom of this mystery. For now, I don't think it really makes a difference, one way or the other."

"I suppose you're right. Either it's aliens or it's not. That changes nothing about how we go about this, does it?"

"Not that I can see."

●●●

"Anna's not buying the whole alien premise, is she?" Mike asked.

"Not any part of it," I said.

"I can't say that I blame her."

"Nor can I. Have you ever run across anything like this at the FBI?"

"I've had some bizarre cases, which is to be expected when you're dealing with mass murderers. But no, nothing that had these elements."

"That's too bad."

"I tried to look at this logically, especially the time thing," Mike said. "If you were correct in your assessment of the time, and Anna was also correct, the logical conclusion had to be what we discussed."

"I don't disagree. She's convinced that my opinion of what happened to me has to be wrong. And who knows, she may be right. It could all be makeup and technology and somebody fucking with us."

"Strangely, that would actually be comforting."

"It would," I said. "What does that say about where we're at?"

"Ha, quite a lot."

"Are you going to try a controlled experience?" I asked.

"Yeah. Thinking about doing it tonight—nothing better to do."

"Keep me in the loop. And be careful."

"Of course."

No matter where this led, it felt right having Mike around again.

●●●

"Just out of curiosity, I set a stopwatch right before I made my attempt."

It was the next day, and Mike was recapping his experience.

"And how long was it?" I asked.

"Just under three hours."

"Wow! That must have been exhausting."

"That's the weird thing," he noted. "I felt like I had just gotten 'there,' wherever 'there' was."

"That's exactly how I felt," I said.

"I know. And so, as soon as I made contact, I started counting in my head. You know, from one to sixty. When I got to sixty-one the first time, I started over at two, then three, etc. That way, I could try to keep track of time while I looked around."

"Brilliant! Although at some point during the three hours, I assume you gave up."

"No. I kept going. And I got to…"

I waited for him to continue. In vain.

"Well, was that just a pause for dramatic effect?"

"Sort of," he laughed. "But more because I can't really believe what I'm about to say."

"And that is?"

"Seven and one-half minutes."

My turn to be silent. The pause seemed endless. Then I said, "Let me get this straight—you experienced just over seven minutes, but the stopwatch clocked almost three hours?"

"That's exactly what I'm telling you."

"Holy shit! Despite what Anna might say, that cannot be a coincidence!"

"I agree."

"So," I said, scrambling to open the calculator app on my phone and trying not to accidentally disconnect the call. "If I said I was gone about two and a half minutes, while Anna said it was an hour, and you were gone seven and a half minutes while your stopwatch said about three hours, that means…"

"I did the same thing you're doing and got about one of our days for every hour in the other place."

"Which means," I said as I continued to calculate in my head, "if we were gone for three days back then, it was…" I stopped as the calculation hit home.

"Yeah," Mike said, "only three hours in whatever place we were being held."

"Holy…fucking…shit," was all I could murmur.

"I couldn't have said it better myself," Mike said.

"Where the hell were we?" I asked, not expecting an answer that made any sense.

"That seems to be the question of the day."

"Anna will never believe this," I said, as I worried about the ramifications.

"There's not really any denying it, but I could see it being a problem for her."

"Oh, there could definitely be a way of denying it," I said. "She'll just say you must have become confused, trying to count for that long while also trying to gather as much information as possible. No, denying it is definitely a possibility. Although, in the long run, it shouldn't make any difference whether or not she believes it."

"Yeah, you're right. It shouldn't."

I pushed that line of thought from my mind and refocused.

"So, were you able to gather any useful intel?"

"Useful intel?" he laughed. "And you talked about me watching Marvel movies. It sounds like you've been watching spy movies."

I laughed and said, "I won't deny it. So, answer the question."

"Yes, sir," he spat out. "In my recon, I observed the following: I appeared to be in a dwelling of some sort. It matched the description of what you thought of as its house. I remained quiet in its mind as I continued my count. It seemed to be relaxing when it suddenly walked to what appeared to be a blank space on a wall. It reached a hand out. This time didn't feel as much like 'my' hand as the last time. I surmised it was because I was intentionally in stealth mode. As the hand reached toward the wall, a large screen appeared, as a portion of the wall itself seemed to melt away. The screen displayed symbols that I didn't recognize, and the hand pressed a series of these symbols. After that, the screen changed to a grid pattern in which symbols or numbers appeared on some, but not all, of the spaces. It reminded me of the calendar program on my computer. It was reviewing the grid, and our eyes landed on a specific rectangle. The hand reached out and tapped it, which didn't cause anything to change on the screen, but it did cause the thing whose head I was in to talk to itself. I couldn't understand the spoken words, but it also thought something. To me, it came across as 'only twenty-four luni-chrons until we go to dimension two and the place my ancestors tried to mold. And the home of my one failure.' Just as you had said, it seemed I could understand if I was in its head, but not otherwise. Then it made a notation on the screen, turned it off, and I was back home."

"Whoa. That's a lot to take in."

"It is. It would be helpful if we could read whatever language that was.”

“It certainly would,” I said. “But even so, based on what you thought it thought, it seems that the grid was some sort of calendar.”

“I agree,” Mike stated. “I made a quick sketch of the grid and tried to recreate the symbols as best I could. I’ll see what I’m able to figure out. So, if it is a calendar, what are twenty-four luni-chrons? And where is dimension two?”

“I think we have to assume that a ‘luni-chron’ is some sort of time reference. Especially if we’re being consistent with what I thought a ‘chron’ was in my experience.”

“Yeah. If a ‘chron’ was a minute, as you originally thought, a ‘luni-chron’ has to be some multiple of a minute, don’t you think?”

“That makes sense, I guess,” my uncertainty apparent. “What the hell is a ‘luni?’”

“It sounds a lot like ‘lunatic,’ which is exactly what most people are going to think we are,” he said.

I laughed. “And it would be hard to disagree with them.” After a pause, I said, “But you might be onto something.”

“What’s that?”

“In older times, a ‘lunatic’ was someone whose madness was believed to rise and fall with the full moon,” I said, my fingers tracing an idle circle in the air. “So, in a way, the moon served as a sort of timekeeping device.”

"Interesting," he murmured, his gaze sharpening. "So, could 'twenty-four luni-chrons' be tied to the moon's phases?"

"Possibly," I replied. "But the real question is—which moon are we talking about? Or how many? And from what vantage point?"

He slumped back in his chair, pinching the bridge of his nose. "Fuck if I know. My head's starting to feel like it's in a vice."

"Yeah, I agree. Let's give it a rest for now," I suggested. Instantly, I could feel him relax.

"All right. I'll talk to you in a couple of days."

"Yep," I said as we disconnected the call. To myself, I thought, *I hope we have a couple of days.*

●●●

My mind refused to let go of something Mike had said: "dimension two and the place my ancestors tried to mold. And the home of my one failure."

That statement kept tickling the deep recesses of my brain, and I couldn't help but try to recall why. I brought up some of my previous research and, as I read, the recollection revealed itself. There were numerous theories about beings, either from another world, galaxy, or dimension, coming to this planet in antiquity. People worshipped them as gods because of their perceived powers. Their powers could very easily have been technology. Technology was unfamiliar to the ancient peoples of Earth, who would understandably confuse it with magic. To paraphrase Arthur C. Clarke, magic is merely technology that is not understood. Hell, the fax machine is still magic to me.

Granted, the theories about those beings were far from mainstream reasoning. Many have characterized them as being crackpot theories. Anna would say they're the easy way out.

But what if? Others would most likely deem our theory about our kidnapper's non-local origin, and the time disparity between his location and our own, as crackpot theories. I'm unfamiliar with the math, but could it be that, unlike two wrongs don't make a right, two crackpot theories working together equal the truth? Maybe, just maybe, some of those theories about the Gods contain a kernel of truth. And if they do, could my home planet be in dimension two and "the place my ancestors tried to mold?" By some accounts, the Gods provided the seeds of civilization, so maybe.

And then there's "the home of my one failure." Could it be? Could the reference be to Mike, Pete, and me? We had both seen what happened to beings caught in that cube. Their life energy was sucked from their bodies, they unceremoniously died, and their bodies were discarded as if trash. But all three of us walked away, mostly unscathed. Could that failure still weigh on its mind after all this time, even factoring in the time difference?

I strongly believed the answer to that question was "Yes!"

And that meant it was coming back. Back to the scene of its failure.

We had twenty-four luni-chrons to figure this out.

●●●

The level of excitement I could feel from Mike was totally unexpected, even before he'd said a word.

"Have some news?" I said.

"You're doing that thing, aren't you?" he said.

"I am. Spill it."

"Spoilsport," he commented before continuing. "I had stared at my sketch of the grid and its symbols for what seemed like days. Then I had a great idea, if I say so myself."

I could tell he was getting back at me for spoiling his surprise, so I let him have his moment.

"OK, I'm sorry for spoiling your surprise, but the suspense is killing me," I admitted.

"Good," he said as he laughed. "I have a friend at the FBI who told me about some super-secret proprietary computer thing called AI. Artificial Intelligence. It's supposed to be way ahead of anything being used by us mere mortals. So I sent my sketch, together with a synopsis of our theory, to her. She ran it through her program and got some interesting results."

"Please, don't make me beg," I pleaded.

"OK, OK. According to the AI calculations, the grid was a calendar! And somehow it concluded that twenty-four luni-chrons were equal to twenty-four hours, in whatever place is being referenced. So, that means twenty-four hours over there is the same as twenty-four days here. Which means that we have twenty-four days from my experience before it goes back to dimension two."

"I think you mean 'comes back' to dimension two," I said.

"Comes back? What are you talking about?"

"I think I know where it's going," I said.

"Explain."

I did.

●●●

After listening to my discourse, all Mike could say was, "Holy crap."

"Of course, I could be totally wrong," I submitted.

"You could be, but I don't think so. It all kind of comes together, like puzzle pieces."

"So, if this is all correct and we have, what, about twenty-two days left before it gets here, what are we going to do?"

I could feel his law enforcement officer mode kick in. "The only thing we can do," he said. "We have no choice but to face this thing head-on. We think we know when it's coming and where it's going to be, so that gives us a minor advantage. I just hope it shares one trait with humans.”

I took the bait and asked. “What's that?”

“Being a creature of habit.”

# CHAPTER 34
# TEMPTING THE VOLCANO

The chime of the doorbell shot through me, and I flung the door open without hesitation. I'd been waiting for what felt like forever—like a kid straining to hear reindeer hooves on the roof. But then, my grip on time has never been the most reliable.

And there he stood. Mike Plotkin. Real, solid, smiling at me with the same warmth I felt breaking across my own face. My brother- from-another-mother, back at last.

He crossed the threshold, and we folded into each other's arms, the years melting away.

I felt the surge of energy course through my body and into his. He must have felt the same, as we were unable to release, as if melded together by electricity. I could no longer see or feel him, either physically or emotionally. Instead, I was looking at what had to be the computer screen he had described in his last experience with the kidnapper. We were studying the schematics for a three-dimensional cube, and our hands were manipulating the image, turning and expanding it. I thought, *Explain.* I could feel Mike join as we both repeated, *Explain,* in our shared mind. The being spoke, and together Mike and I thought, *Think.* Instead of its talking, the explanation poured directly into our one mind. *This is the schematic for the updated inter-dimensional bio cube. These will serve as energy traps for my feast, positioned throughout Dimension Number Two's so-called Earth. They each contain all that is required to fulfill my needs.* We could feel as the being struggled to regain control, but Mike and I held on. It was like riding a mental bucking bronco. *It matters not what you know of this. If you dare to enter again, you will not escape. Now, BE GONE!*

Our eight seconds expired, and as soon as we finished thinking the last word, the pulsating energy stopped, and we released our grip on each other, forcing us to stagger backward. We steadied ourselves and stared at each other. Suddenly, we both burst out in uncontrollable laughter.

Anna, who had watched the episode, said, "What the hell was that? Your hair was standing on end, and you were motionless for like ten minutes."

When we could again control ourselves, we closed the door and walked to the nearest seating.

"Well?" Anna's impatience was showing.

"As soon as we touched, something transported us to a meeting with the kidnapper," I explained. "It was our two minds, acting as one, against its mind."

"And we were able to exert some control," Mike said, as he got up to embrace Anna.

We told her everything we had just experienced, and I could feel her disbelief waver for a microsecond before returning in full force.

"And you both thought it was funny?"

"No," I said. "It was just the release of tension."

"And relief," Mike added.

"So," Anna continued, "it knows who you are. And it sounds like it knows you're planning on going to it. Doesn't that alarm you?"

"You'd think it should, wouldn't you?" I asked.

"Yes, I would!" she replied.

"And to a certain degree, it does. But not as much as I might have thought before this happened."

"Why?" Anna asked.

"Because I felt something else." I turned to Mike, my gaze locking with his. "And with our one-mind connection, I'm willing to bet you felt it too—didn't you?"

"I did," he answered.

"And that was?" Anna prodded.

Together, Mike and I said, "Fear."

●●●

We spent the rest of the evening catching up on each other's lives over the past two decades. We pointedly avoided the incident at the front door. For me, it was to avoid making Anna too uncomfortable. I can't speak as to Mike's motivation, but I could guess that he was following my lead, having assumed I knew my wife well enough to know how to handle the situation.

As Anna and I were getting into bed, she said, "I thought you said Mike was a fairly quiet guy. Taciturn may have been the word you used."

"My recollection is that he usually was," I responded.

"Hmm. He seemed pretty talkative tonight."

"And the last few times I've spoken to him on the phone, as well," I noted.

"Interesting," she said. "Maybe he's loosening up a bit."

"Maybe," I said, "but I think it's more a matter of his being comfortable around us, and me in particular, no offense."

"I get that," she said. "You've known each other for most of your lives, even if you haven't seen or spoken to each other for a long time. With some people, you can just go on from where you left off, no matter how long ago it was."

"That's definitely the case with Mike and me," I agreed. "I think it might also be something else."

"Don't keep me waiting," she said through a yawn.

"I think working on this fifty-year-old mystery has also energized him. I got the feeling he's missed the challenge."

"I suppose that makes sense. It's what he did every day for years. Quitting cold-turkey can be tough."

"Let's hope this is enough of a fix for him," I said, as I stifled a yawn of my own.

●●●

The next day, we convened at the breakfast table.

"So," I opened, "if our calculations have been correct, we have about ten days before our showdown."

"Just so I'm clear," Anna interjected, "you're planning on somehow finding this *person* and confronting him or her? Is that correct?"

Ignoring her pointed reference to the *person*, I said, "Yes. I think that's accurate."

"And then…what?" Addressing Mike, she continued, "Are you going to arrest him? Can a retired agent even do that?"

"Well, technically, no. I can't. But, as with any other citizen, I, we, can affect a citizen's arrest. Then I can call in local law enforcement and actual active FBI agents."

That seemed to mollify her, at least for the moment.

"OK," she said. "How do you plan on finding where and when this kidnapper is going to be?"

"This," I began, "is where you might not have quite the level of confidence we do."

"Of that," she said, "I have no doubt. Tell me anyway."

"All right. Since you asked, we are fairly confident we know when the kidnapper will be arriving."

"This is based on your calculation of time differences and what you saw and heard when you were connected?"

I looked at Mike, who saw the pleading in my eyes.

"Yes," he answered, rescuing me.

I could feel the skepticism oozing from her. If I were a betting man, I'd have bet that even Mike could feel it.

"Then what?"

Mike continued. "We're going back to the place where we disappeared. We know it's a location the kidnapper has used before. Also, we got the feeling it's waiting for us, and it's the only place we know of where it could be. So, that location seems to be the only one that makes sense to us."

"So, basically, if all your calculations and surmising are correct, you're planning on walking into something that is most likely a trap?"

"I don't think I'd characterize it quite that way," I said.

"No?" she countered. "How would you characterize it?"

"More like a calculated risk," I said with as much bluster as I could manage, which, admittedly, wasn't a lot.

She sat quietly, assessing both of us. It was like waiting for the pressure in a volcano to reach its peak just before exploding. And then, unexpectantly, it was as if a pressure valve had been released and the magma receded back into the earth.

"I don't suppose there's anything I could say to dissuade you of this cockamamie scheme, is there?"

I reached for her hand, which she accepted. "No. This is something we have to do. It's been festering for fifty years, and we'll probably never get another chance."

"Would that be so bad?" she asked, ever hopeful.

"It's not something either of us could live with," I answered.

She looked at Mike, who nodded in agreement.

Resigned, she said, "All right. What do you need me to do?"

I looked at Mike, who said, "We're going to need a ride."

# CHAPTER 35
# ACT LIKE WE BELONG

We were six days out from our targeted date when we rolled up to our destination, Anna behind the wheel. Mike and I had decided not to take the chance of being intercepted by our unknown tormentor while either of us was driving. Especially with us being together.

Anna pulled into a waiting parking space, and the three of us sat in silence, staring at the imposing structure.

The Elgin Mental Health Center.

Although I could read the words, my mind instantly transformed them to the Northern Illinois Hospital and Asylum for the Insane.

The Asylum. Home to Pete Wilson.

"Are we going to do this?" Mike asked from the back seat of the car.

Unable to avert my gaze from the sign, I replied, "We came all this way. We might as well."

"Guys," she implored, "please take it easy on Pete. I can only imagine what his state of mind is after spending most of his life in there. And then to suddenly see you both. It could be overwhelming."

"We'll do our best," I assured her.

The doorway stretched farther with every step I took, as if retreating into the shadows. I knew it was only my mind twisting reality, mirroring the unease in my chest. Still, dread coiled tighter inside me with every stride. I didn't have to glance at Mike to sense he carried the same weight.

We walked through the double doors into the foyer. On our right was a large reception desk. A large reception desk with nobody behind it.

"Just keep walking," Mike whispered. "Look like we're supposed to be here."

I nodded imperceptively and followed his lead. In a return whisper, I said, "Any idea where we're going?"

"We'll figure it out. First things first. Let's get inside."

We walked another fifty feet, through a faux portico, and saw a staircase on our right. Without hesitation, we turned and bounded up the stairs. At the landing, we faced an imposing-looking metal door. Mike grabbed the handle and tried turning.

Locked.

"Let's keep going upstairs until we find one that's not locked," he said.

As we moved up the stairs, I said, "Did they teach you this criminal stuff at Quantico?"

"Pretty much," he replied. "It's important to know how the other half does what they do. What they didn't teach was basically a matter of reverse engineering."

When we got to the fourth floor, we hit pay dirt. I grasped the handle, found no resistance, and we stepped through the opening into a busy hallway.

There were large rooms with windows into which one could see from the hall. There were other rooms with no windows, some with open doorways. This floor appeared to contain meeting and other multi-purpose rooms. We could see craft tables in some, chairs arranged in a circle in another, and a well-appointed library. Patients and orderlies filled the hallway, moving with purpose toward unseen destinations. They hardly noticed us, aside from the rare passing glance. From the relatively light crowd, it seemed we'd arrived during a lull in the day's routines.

"Can I help you?"

We both came to a skidding halt and spun towards the sound of the voice, where we confronted a young-looking man, apparently of East Indian descent. He was wearing a white lab coat with a name tag: Arthur Singh. Without missing a beat, Mike said, "Oh, thank goodness, Mr. Singh. We must've taken a wrong turn somewhere. We're looking for Pete Wilson."

Mr. Singh smiled as he made no attempt at hiding his assessment of us.

"Do you have a visitor's pass? It's supposed to be displayed in a visible location."

As I fumbled around and shuffled my feet, Mike reached into his pocket and removed a small billfold, which he flicked open to reveal a photo ID emblazoned with the letters "FBI." He took a step towards Mr. Singh, holding the ID up at eye level as he said, "This is a special circumstance, Mr. Singh. I'm sure you understand. We'd like to keep this as low profile as possible, so if you could just direct us to Mr. Wilson, I would be very appreciative."

I could see him churning through the possible scenarios and consequences.

"Mr. Singh? Please, as you might imagine, time is of the essence."

"Very well. Mr. Wilson's room is on the third floor, in the west wing. I'll alert the staff to your arrival."

Mike reached out and gently touched his arm as he leaned nearer to Mr. Singh's ear, creating an intimacy that clearly caused Mr. Singh to feel uncomfortable. Quietly, he said, "Mr. Singh, that would be a mistake. You don't want to interfere with an ongoing investigation, do you? There would be consequences."

I sensed Mr. Singh's relief as Mike stepped back and awaited the reply, his hand inching slowly but noticeably towards his hip, where a concealed weapon would typically hide. I hadn't noticed one before, but nothing would surprise me about Agent Plotkin.

"No, of course not, Mr. Plotkin. I'm sorry, Agent Plotkin."

"Great. We appreciate your help. Just one more thing."

"Yes, sir?"

"What's the room number?"

Immediately, Mr. Singh used the small electronic device hanging from his belt, looked up, and said, "Room 3303W."

"Perfect! We can't thank you enough." As we turned to leave, Mike once again faced Mr. Singh. "Elevator?"

Mr. Singh's arm came up, and he pointed back in the direction from which we had come. Wordlessly, we turned and walked in the indicated direction. We waited for the elevator, stepped in, and, as the doors closed, I let out a long, slow breath.

"That was close," I said.

Mike, still looking straight ahead at the elevator doors, said, "We're not home free just yet."

●●●

3303W.

We faced the door emblazoned with the identification of the room. Neither of us moved.

3303W.

It dared us to knock.

3303W.

It dared us to turn the handle.

3303W.

It dared us to confront our collective past.

I looked at Mike. He nodded. My hand came up and contacted the door.

Once, twice, three times.

"Come in." Muffled. Slightly slurred.

We entered the room and quietly closed the door behind us as we faced the bed, standing side-by-side. Neither of us said a word. We took in the surroundings: a simple dresser, bed, chair, armoire, and desk. On the bed was a man who bore little resemblance to the Pete Wilson I remembered. Balding and disheveled, wearing a stained t-shirt, his sweat pants topped by an overhanging belly reminiscent of the Buddha.

"Hey, Pete," I said quietly. I remembered what Anna had said and was determined to be as gentle as possible.

Mike, also quietly, said, "Hi, Pete."

Slowly, Pete worked his way up to a sitting position. It was painful to watch. His movements were deliberate, and his eyes lacked focus. He sat with his bare feet on the floor, blankly staring at us. He blinked hard, unnaturally, and rubbed his eyes.

"Are you real?"

"We are," I answered.

He painstakingly rose from the bed and shuffled in our direction. He stopped directly in front of us and gently reached out with both hands, one hand for each of our faces. When he realized we were no illusion, his legs gave way and he collapsed onto the floor, sobbing. We joined him there, sharing both his seat and his relief.

●●●

We remained on the floor after our tears had been spent. It was easier for Pete that way.

"If you're really here, why?"

"We need your help, buddy," Mike said.

Showing more awareness of his condition than I would have thought possible, he motioned to himself and said, "My help? How could I possibly help anybody? I can barely help myself."

"Trust us, Pete," I said. "We really need your help."

"Trust you? I can barely trust that you're actually here." He reached out to touch us again, but stopped himself mid-motion. "It's been decades, and I'm just supposed to trust you?" He searched our faces and saw only regret. "Why should I?"

"Because it's us," I said lamely. "And because we might be

able to put to rest any questions about what happened to us."

"Are you talking about our…you know?" It was evident that even thinking about what happened to us was upsetting.

"We are," Mike said. "We might get some closure. Wouldn't you like that?"

"Closure," he said, wistfully. "Closure. What would that even look like? Especially for someone like me? Am I supposed to get out of here and live a 'normal' life, whatever that might be?"

"Are you still hearing the voices?" I asked.

"Shush," he said, as his eyes darted around the room. "We don't talk about that."

"Are you?" I whispered. "It's important."

He leaned forward and whispered, "Sometimes, if I get too close to the park outside. But I've learned not to say anything. And the medicine helps."

"That's good," Mike said. Matching Pete's whisper, he leaned forward and said in as conspiratorial a tone as possible, "I still feel evil, and Jack still feels the emotions of others."

"Really?"

Mike and I both nodded our assent.

"Do you need my help to get rid of these 'abilities'?"

Mike and I shared a quick glance before I said, "Maybe. We're not sure what will happen, but there's a chance."

I didn't want to outright lie to him, but I didn't want to destroy what could be our only chance to get him to help.

"I don't know," he said. "I think I'm getting better. Maybe. I'm afraid to change anything."

"Pete, we can't do this without you," Mike said. "It might be the only chance we'll ever have to get any closure."

"Do what, Mike? You haven't really said."

"That's a really long story," I interjected. "Why don't you come with us, and we'll fill you in?"

"Come with you? Like, outside? Leave this place?"

"Yes. You can stay at my house for a few days. Anna, my wife, would love to meet you. And she's a nurse, so if you have any issues, she'll be able to help."

"I don't know," he said. I could feel his trepidation growing.

"It'll be fun," I said. "Like when we were kids. The three of us having a sleepover."

"Maybe. That could be fun. We had fun when we were kids, didn't we?"

"We sure did," Mike responded. "What do you say? Let's have an adventure."

"You guys won't leave me, will you?"

"Of course not," I said. "We definitely will not leave you."

"All right. Let's have an adventure. I'll pack some stuff. I need to get my meds, and then we'll get permission."

"Leave that to me," Mike said, glancing at me suspiciously.

"Cool. Help me up, please."

●●●

We helped Pete gather up some clothes, stuffing them into a backpack he had in his armoire. Mike went into the bathroom to get his toiletries and medications, and I helped him change into clothing more appropriate to being outside.

"Ready?" I asked.

"I guess so."

"You're going to be fine, Pete," Mike assured him. "Let's go."

We opened the door to find an empty hallway, trying not to be too obvious about the nature of our excursion. Pete shuffled along as we casually walked to the elevator. We passed other patients, each of whom matched Pete's shuffle and addressed him by name. Pete responded in kind, introducing us as "old friends" and telling them he was going on an adventure. We became a little worried about that until the patients nodded, said "cool," and continued shuffling along.

The doors of the elevator opened on the first floor and

revealed the reception desk, along with the receptionist, busy with a visitor. We made an immediate turn out of the elevator and stopped behind a wall. As soon as the visitor left, Mike nodded at me and strode to the receptionist, a twenty-something woman wearing what must have been the worker's lab coat uniform. Her name, Suzanne, appeared on her name tag. As Mike approached, she looked up and presented him with a dazzling smile.

"Hi, Suzanne. How are you today?"

"I'm fine. Thank you. How may I help you?"

He removed his billfold and presented his FBI credentials as he quietly said, "Suzanne, who is the head administrator?"

Mimicking his quiet tone, she said, "That would be Dr. Gonzales."

"Great. I'll need you to get Dr. Gonzales."

She reached for the phone as she said, "I'll call her."

Mike's hand shot out and stifled the call. "No. I need you to bring her here. I'll wait."

"I don't know. I really shouldn't leave the desk alone."

"I know someone left it alone before," he said. As she opened her mouth to reply, he said, "It's OK. I won't tell. And it won't be left alone. I'll wait right here." Seeing her hesitancy, he said, "Suzanne, it's important. Please?"

"All right. Wait right here. I'll be back in a moment."

As she left her post, I saw Mike motion behind his back for us to leave.

"OK, Pete. Let's go."

I held him by the elbow and led him out the front door. As we passed the reception desk, he looked at Mike, who gave him the thumbs up. Trying to hurry, but not appear as if we were doing so, was a feat not easily accomplished, and I wasn't certain we were successful. All I know is that we made it outside with nobody screaming for us to stop.

Anna must have seen us come out of the building because our feet hadn't yet touched the parking lot as she pulled up and said, "Get in." As we did so, Mike came running out, opened the front passenger door, and jumped in.

"Let's go," he said.

Anna saw Pete had not yet buckled his seat belt and said, "Let's get Pete buckled in."

Mike looked at her and said, "Drive, please. We'll get him buckled on the way."

Understanding dawned, and the accelerator met the floor, shooting us out of the parking lot and on our way.

# CHAPTER 36
# LET'S PROVE EVERYBODY WRONG

After we arrived at our house, we got Pete settled in one of the guest rooms. Mike was upstairs helping him unpack and trying to make him feel at home. I was downstairs in the kitchen with Anna.

"Are you telling me you kidnapped him!?!"

"No. No. Definitely not. He came willingly."

"Is he even competent enough to make that decision?"

"I think he is. We conversed, he asked questions, and then he agreed to come."

"Did you explain what was really going on?"

"Well, not exactly. We told him it was a long story, and we'd tell him later. We'll tell him tomorrow."

"Damn it, Jack. This is crazy!"

"No, it's not! Desperate, maybe, but not crazy. I'm convinced of it."

Her offensive broke, her movements stalling. I'm certain it was then she recognized the full measure of my commitment.

"Just promise me that if he changes his mind, you won't force him to go along. Promise me."

"I promise. We will not force him to go along."

"Thank you."

●●●

We'd asked Pete what he wanted for dinner, and his answer was, "Pizza. Really good Chicago pizza. With sausage and pepperoni."

A man after my own heart.

During dinner, we engaged him in idle chitchat. I could tell that Anna was assessing his condition as we interacted. Accustomed to going to bed early, Pete was struggling to stay awake, so we assured him it was okay, said our good-nights, and Anna helped him to get ready.

When she came back downstairs, we spoke in hushed tones.

"So," I said, "what do you think of his mental acuity?"

"It's actually better than I thought it would be. I think a lot of his fuzziness is because of the medication."

"I'm glad to hear you say that," Mike said.

"Why is that?" asked Anna.

"Because we need him off his meds and back to full mental capacity."

"You can't be serious! He's on anti-psychotics, anti-depressants, and anti-hallucinogens. Taking him off those meds is going to result in a psychotic break! That's the last thing you want!"

"I appreciate that, but in this case, I don't think it's accurate. He's on those drugs because when he first showed up to his therapist, nobody believed that what he was experiencing was real. They were out of their depth and, rather than considering that he was telling the truth, had no clue what to do. The answer back then, and maybe even today, I don't know, was to load him up with drugs. They'd have done the same thing to us if we'd been honest and told them what we were experiencing. He'll be better off without them."

"How can you be so sure? You're not a doctor," Anna said.

"Anna, in my line of work, I've dealt with all types of mental illnesses. I've seen what real psychotics look like and know full well what they're capable of. Pete is not like that. He's just been overmedicated for way too long. And we need him sharp. At least as sharp as he can be in the next five days."

Anna looked at me as if I could somehow talk some sense into Mike. I could only shrug and say, "Let's wean him off. Maybe give him some sort of placebo. You'll be here to monitor the situation. If you think he's showing signs of real psychosis, then we get him back on his meds."

"I can't believe I'm saying this. I'll agree, provided you two agree to tell him exactly what's going on. If he's being duped, I'm out."

"Agreed. Thank you," I said.

As she stood to remove herself from our presence, she said,

"This is complete insanity. Don't thank me just yet. "

●●●

"You want me to stop taking my meds?"

"We do," I said. "They only put you on those medications because nobody believed you were really hearing voices. We know better."

"I don't know. What will happen to me without them?" I could feel his fear rising and watched as his eyes darted around the room.

This not being my or Mike's area of expertise, we looked to Anna for guidance.

"Pete," she said, exhibiting her bedside manner, "I think you'll be just fine. If, as the boys say, they only prescribed you the medication because they didn't believe you were hearing voices, then they misdiagnosed you. So, the meds wouldn't be proper for your condition."

"And what condition is that?" he asked.

"Well, Pete, I'm not certain there actually is a condition," she answered.

"Pete," Mike said, "they'd have done the same thing to us if anybody had any idea what we were going through."

Mike paused, and I could almost see the thought form.

"It's ironic, isn't it?"

248

"What's that, Mike?"

"The only reason you received treatment was that, of the three of us, you were the only one with a mother who cared enough to want to help."

The truth of the statement hit me like a gut punch. "Shit. I never looked at it like that," I said. "But damn, it's accurate."

"Wow," Anna said. "That's quite a revelation, Mike. It never occurred to me."

"It hadn't occurred to me until now either," Mike admitted. "Is life fucked up, or what?"

"Yeah, I'd have to say it is. It most definitely is," I agreed.

"So, what do you say, Pete?" Mike asked.

"I still don't know. What if you're wrong?"

"How's this?" Anna interjected. "What if, instead of just cutting off your meds, we cut down the dosage for the next couple of days? Will that work for you?"

I could feel how much trust Pete had in Anna. He confirmed it when he said, "That sounds like a good compromise, Anna. Let's do that. Thank you."

"Of course," she said as she reached out and patted his shoulder. "I'll get the pills and start cutting them."

As she left to perform her stated duties, I could see Pete's eyes follow her every movement.

"Don't worry, Pete. Anna won't let anything bad happen to you."

"I know," he said. "Jack, you're one lucky son-of-a-bitch." It was the first time I'd seen a hint of the old Pete.

"No argument from me, Pete. None."

Having made the decision to cut back on his meds, Pete decided it was time to get more information. The moment Mike and I had been dreading.

"So, boys," he said, "I'm not sure how long I can stay awake. Why am I here?"

Mike said, "Get comfortable. This is going to take a while."

●●●

We started from the beginning and went through everything we'd experienced or theorized to the time we'd gone to get Pete. It took hours. During the recitation, we took a few breaks, mainly to use the restroom, get food and drink, and keep Pete awake and as focused as possible. Anna came and went. But Mike and I were determined to stay together through the entire discourse. When we'd finished, we let the silence wash over us.

"Any thoughts?" I asked.

Pete roused himself, and I could feel him focus. "Oh yeah. I have thoughts. My main thought being, 'How the hell was I the one locked up and not the two of you?' That is genuinely and completely crazy. Certifiable. You both should have been my roommates."

"A reasonable conclusion that I believe Anna shares with you," I noted.

"At least one person here is sane," Pete said.

There wasn't much more to be said on the subject, so we didn't. We'd each disappeared into our own worlds until Pete said, "Listen, I'm still a little fuzzy. So, just to be clear, you want us to find this 'being' and confront him, or it, and do what?"

"We're not sure yet," Mike admitted. "But I'm sure it will become clear as time goes on."

Even in his current condition, that struck Pete as odd. "Is this how the FBI operates?" he asked.

"More often than you'd think."

"Well, all I can say is, I'm glad we cut back on my meds. I know it's only been a day, but I'm already feeling like I can concentrate and think better. And after that story, I realize that a clear head is really going to come in handy."

"Am I hearing what I think I just heard?" I said.

Pete smiled and said, "I spent a lot of time being really pissed at you both. Pissed and jealous. I was very conflicted. I wanted you both to be happy, but suffer because of what happened to me. It wasn't your fault, but I needed to blame someone, and that was the two of you. I know it's been a few decades since we've interacted, but you guys are still the best friends and closest thing to family I've ever had, or will ever have. So, I got over it. I also know that neither of you would come up with something this bat-shit-crazy unless you were totally convinced it was true. So, what the hell? Everybody already thinks I'm crazy. Let's prove them wrong."

He paused and studied both of us, an unexpected twinkle in his eye. "Or right."

# CHAPTER 37
# ANNA'S JOURNAL ENTRY #3

*So, I may or may not be complicit in a kidnapping.*

*Jack and Mike got Pete out of the institution, and they both swore that Pete left voluntarily. Even so, I'm not sure how much of the situation Pete understood. Anyway, Jack has promised to explain everything to Pete and not force him into anything, and I can trust him to follow through.*

*Against my better judgment, I agreed to monitor Pete's withdrawal from his medications. Jack and Mike were so convinced that Pete was misdiagnosed that they persuaded me to go along. They agreed that, if I felt Pete needed to go back on his meds, they wouldn't fight it. I hate to admit it, but they were right. Pete has really started to come around and become more of himself. And that's just from an initial cutting down on the meds, not from totally cutting them off.*

*It's got me thinking: If they were right about Pete's hearing the voices and being misdiagnosed, what else could they have gotten right? I'm not saying that the whole alien hypothesis is correct, but maybe something is going on.*

*I'll try to maintain an open mind. For now.*

# CHAPTER 38
# PLANNING FOR THE UNKNOWN

"What's interesting to me," Anna said when we had some privacy, "is what this whole thing has meant to both Pete and Mike."

"What do you mean?"

"You know how you thought Mike needed the challenge again? Something to give him purpose?"

"Yeah."

"I think Pete has that in common with him. I mean, some of it might relate to his reduced medication, but he seems more aware. Involved. Competent. Like having this thing to do with you guys has given him purpose for what might be the first time in his life."

I hadn't thought about it in those terms, but now that it had been pointed out, I saw it clearly.

"You're right," I said. "Since Mike retired, he has that in common with Pete. In that regard, I guess I'm the odd man out."

"You say that as if it's a bad thing. It's not. You still have your work."

"And you," I said.

She gave me a kiss and said, "That's sweet. Don't get all mushy on me."

I laughed and said, "I'll try to keep it under control. Speaking of Pete's meds, what do you think of his decision to go completely off them?"

"Actually, having seen the difference in him from just going to a half dosage after one day, I'll be honest enough to say you guys were right. Don't let it go to your head."

Smiling, I wrapped her in my arms and squeezed. "I'll try. Now, let's go to bed."

●●●

We were at T-minus four days. How the hell does one prepare for the complete unknown?

●●●

We talked incessantly. About the inter-dimensional bio cube. The purse. The bracelet. And about what awaited us. And how to press our attack. What advantage could we possibly hope to find against what we perceived to be a higher intelligence with advanced technology?

Like the mostly dead Dread Pirate Roberts on the bridge overlooking the castle, we listed our assets, or, in our case, possible assets: surprise (maybe); knowledge (limited); unity (for whatever it was worth); our three acquired "abilities." That seemed to exhaust the list.

"Wait a minute," Mike encouraged. "Unity. That might

actually be something."

"How?" asked Pete.

"When I first got here, Jack and I hugged. As soon as we did, we were thrown into an encounter with the kidnapper."

"I remember you telling me about it," Pete acknowledged.

"Yeah. The difference between that and our separate encounters was that we were able to exert some control over the being. It didn't last long, but it had to fight to get rid of us."

"So," I continued, "with the three of us working together, we should be able to exert even more control. Maybe for long enough to influence its actions."

"Maybe." Mike's gaze slid to Pete. "We're counting on you in there. Concentrate, and if you catch either of our voices in your head, don't question it—just follow."

"I'll give it my best. I promise."

"That's all we can ask," I said.

# CHAPTER 39
# TIME TO USE OUR HEADS

T-minus zero.

The day I had both anticipated and dreaded was upon us. Had this been an action movie, we would have spent at least two scenes getting our uniforms and weaponry battle-ready while appropriately evocative music blared from the speakers.

Alas, it was just us and the all-encompassing silence.

●●●

At ten o'clock a.m., Anna drove us to The Park. Instead of pulling into the parking lot, we drove to Campbell Avenue, the side street nearest our destination. I felt as if I didn't want to be seen. Something about three grown men hanging out in a school park during broad daylight. It felt like putting the shoe on the other foot, so to speak.

We got out of the car, and Anna gave both Mike and Pete wordless hugs. They walked away to afford us some privacy.

"Don't hang around. I don't know how long we'll be, given the time discrepancy and all," I said.

"All right." She hesitated before speaking again. "Are you sure about this, Jack? It's not too late to give it up."

I turned to where Mike and Pete had stopped, waiting.

"Yes, it is," I responded. "Even if I wanted to, I couldn't now. There's too much riding on this. We'll be fine. I promise."

She ignored the promise she knew was beyond my ability to keep and instead gave me a long, hard embrace. "Be careful. I love you."

"Love you too."

●●●

"So, what now?" I asked as I approached my compatriots.

"Who knows?" Mike responded. "This is unfamiliar territory for us all."

"Let's keep walking to the spot." Pete contributed.

We walked, stopped at what we all remembered as being "the spot," and waited. When nobody felt anything, we walked some more. We covered the entire park, except for the playground.

"We might as well go in there, too," I suggested.

We did, even stopping to sit on the swings.

"Could we have miscalculated?" I asked.

"It's possible," Mike said. "We were basing the whole timing thing on an assumption."

"And you know what they say about that," Pete said.

"Let's do another circuit," Mike suggested.

We did two more.

"Well, let's not make this a total waste of time," Pete said. "Who's up for a bite to eat?"

"Might as well," I replied.

Experiencing a strong sense of déjà vu, we walked to Touhy Avenue in search of a place to eat. Our old haunts were gone, but a couple of decent replacements existed.

●●●

There was no full plate of fries left on the table at this meeting. We were hungry, and we didn't hold back. For a few minutes, we were kids again, just having a good time. If nothing else came from this foolishness, it was still worth it.

●●●

We walked back to the park, not having any other way to go about instituting our plan. As we passed what had once been the home of little Billy Roberts, I wondered to myself if he still lived there, then realized I was probably the only person in the neighborhood from back in the day who still lived in their childhood home. No doubt Billy's parents were long dead by now. I hoped they were able to find happiness, either together or with new partners, although experience had taught me that Mr. Roberts probably went on to make a new partner miserable.

●●●

By late afternoon, the sun had dipped low, and my legs ached as if we'd marched through a marathon. Pete lagged behind, his face flushed, each step heavier than the last—he hadn't pushed himself this hard since our old park days. When we stumbled upon a place that felt like a destination, we sank down gratefully. Pete's breathing came rough and uneven, but already the pause was giving him some relief.

"How much longer are we going to give this?" Pete asked. "Much more walking and you guys are going to have to carry me."

"Yeah, well, that's not happening," I said. "I'd welcome someone to carry me at this point." Turning to Mike, I said, "What do you think?"

"I don't know. I suppose it's possible we miscalculated. We still have hours of daylight, but I'm beginning to feel as if this was a mistake."

"Do you guys want to call it for today? If it shows up, it seems it stays for a while. We could try again tomorrow."

Before either of them could answer, we saw Anna drive up and park. As she exited the car, I stood and told the others I'd be right back. Anna and I walked towards one another, meeting on the grass about fifty yards from where Mike and Pete still sat. After we hugged in greeting, she said, "Sitting at home was driving me crazy. How's it going?"

"It's not," I said. "There's been nothing. We've walked this entire park at least a dozen times. Pete was struggling, so we just sat and took a break, trying to decide whether or not to call it a day. Maybe come back tomorrow."

"That sounds like a…" She didn't get to finish her statement because of the shouts from Mike and Pete.

The emotions coming from both of them overwhelmed me, and I turned to find Pete bent over, covering his ears like he always did when he heard the voices. Turning to Anna, I hurriedly said, "Don't come any closer," and ran back to my friends. Anna remained motionless and watched.

I rushed over, grabbed Pete by the shoulders, and tried to still him, but he just kept rocking back and forth, chanting, "Make it stop, make it stop." His eyes were wide, unfocused. I looked at Mike. "You feel it too, don't you?" His nod was sharp, almost pained. "Then how the hell do we get in?"

"It mentioned something about this being an energy trap, or something," Mike said. "Do you remember?"

"Yeah, when you got to the house and we engaged it together. If it's a trap, why haven't we sprung it?"

"I don't know, but we have got to do something," Mike responded.

He stood and searched our surroundings as I remained bent over at Pete's side. I could feel something change in Mike's emotional energy and looked up at him.

"We have to use our heads," he said.

"I'm thinking as hard as I can at the moment," I said, annoyed.

Mike bent down and joined me. "No, that's not what I mean. Do you remember when I told you about my last experience with the kidnapper?"

"Sort of. What is it?" I said, not trying to hide the urgency in my voice.

"It had this round thing with the three-spoked symbol. Like a branding iron."

"I remember. What about it?"

"It was some kind of key. It used it to turn on the T-shaped pillar, and it walked through. What if we have a key?"

"That would be amazing, but I'm pretty sure I don't have one, and you've certainly never mentioned having one."

Pete continued to mutter, and I sensed his struggle to maintain control. I placed my hand on his back and said, "Hang in there. We're working on it."

"Because I didn't put it together before." He reached out and touched my head. "The streaks in our hair. They're the key."

I was astounded. "Damn! If we put our heads together in the right formation, we'll form the same pattern as the branding iron thing."

"I think so."

He kneeled down and joined us. I looked up and turned to see Anna observing. When she saw me make eye contact, she started moving towards us. I held up my hand and shouted. "No. Stay there. We're OK."

Mike and I arranged ourselves around Pete, who was already kneeling with his head down towards the ground. We mimicked his position until our heads were touching. We couldn't get quite the correct positioning, so we asked Pete to pick his head up off the ground. Once our heads were at the same level, Mike and I moved forward, our heads meeting Pete's. Nothing happened until we made some slight adjustments, and our hair streaks touched, forming the desired pattern.

A golden light burst forth from our heads, shooting forward and forming the three-spoke pattern. Once fully formed, the pattern slowly spun in a clockwise direction, stopped after a quarter rotation, and exploded in a blinding burst of golden energy.

●●●

We remained in the kneeling position, but were no longer outdoors. Pete continued to rock while covering his ears, saying, "It's louder! They're right here."

Mike and I stood and took in our surroundings. We were inside an inter-dimensional bio cube. None of the swirling lights we had seen before were visible. No person or being waited to pounce. We were alone.

"What the fuck is going on?"

Mike continued to check out the cube as he said, "I have no idea."

Pete continued to moan and rock on the floor.

"Why aren't we stuck to the floor?" I asked.

Mike picked his feet up, confirming. "Maybe it's because we had a key and we haven't activated the trap protocols?"

"Makes as much sense as anything else," I said.

I jumped as Pete shouted, "Stop! Just stop! One at a time. Please!"

I could feel his instant calmness as he looked up, stood, and said, "Thank you."

"What is it?" asked Mike.

"The voices. So strong in here. But they stopped when I shouted."

This entire experience was baffling, and I said as much as we moved about the cube and explored.

"Stop!"

We looked at Pete, who had just shouted the directive.

"Are they back?" Mike asked.

"No. Well, yes. Sort of. But I meant that for the two of you. Don't touch anything."

Immediately, Mike and I stood still, hands at our sides.

"Why? What is it?" I inquired.

"One of the voices is talking to me. He, it's a he, says that he's been chosen as the spokesperson. They don't want us doing anything until they can explain some things."

"That sounds like a great idea," Mike said. "But please ask him to hurry and explain before the owner of this cube makes a visit."

# CHAPTER 40
# SURPRISES

"They're the essence of the individuals whose energy has been consumed in this cube. Something about not being able to destroy energy, only transform it. They're the transformed remnants of those peoples', or beings', energy."

"Does the cube's owner know they're here?" asked Mike.

It was apparent that Pete was communicating with the spokesperson, so we waited. ·

"No. And they'd like to keep it that way, if possible."

"Understood."

"Speaking of the owner of this thing," I said, "what is it?"

"They call it a Morphosisapien, which means 'a shape-shifting life sap.'"

"Sounds appropriate," I noted. "Will 'Morpho' be back soon?"

"They won't see it coming. He will though—he always comes back. He, and it is a he, appears within minutes of a trap going off, no matter where he's stationed or what he's doing. There are thousands of these scattered worldwide. Even without you springing it, the system already knows. It knows something's gone wrong."

"Then your friends better give us some useful information very soon," Mike said. "What do they think we can do?"

"They're not sure. One thing they know is that Morpho still holds a grudge against us. We're the only proposed victims to have escaped, and for him, it's only been a couple of our years since it happened. So it's almost like it happened yesterday."

Mike looked at me, the hint of a smile visible. "At least we were right about the time thing."

"It's the small victories that count," I said.

"Any known vulnerabilities?" Mike asked.

"Whatever we used to fight it back then. At one point, we held hands, and our bond, both physical and emotional, was the thing that seemed to frustrate him."

"It would sure be nice if we could remember anything that happened," I said.

Mike was about to say something when the opening in the T-pillar shimmered and the Morphosisapien took a step forward. I could feel its surprise as it first laid eyes upon us.

●●●

He towered over us—easily seven feet tall, massive by human standards. I couldn't make out every detail of his form at first, only that he was bipedal. But the moment his eyes fell on us, his shape shifted into something else entirely—a muscular, bird-headed human hybrid. He was the exact likeness of the carvings Mike and I had studied.

"It took that shape because its ancestors found it to be the most intimidating," Pete said, obviously getting information from his new voice friend.

"We are not the same humans your ancestors came to control," Mike said. I could feel him striving to control his fear and appear calm.

"No, you are not," he said in a booming voice meant to intimidate.

"You speak English," I sputtered.

"I speak any language I choose," he said as he walked to a table on which sat a cradle for the purse he was carrying. He placed the purse in its cradle and pressed a colored petal on the bracelet he wore, changing the color of the lights. Seemingly ignoring us, he said, "I've been looking forward to seeing you all again."

"Really?" Mike said as he stealthily approached the table. "Why is that?"

Turning to face Mike, he laughed and said, "Because I am not used to failure. It's been weighing on my mind."

Quick as a crack of lightning, he took a step towards Mike, and with a sweep of his powerful arm, sent him flying against a far wall, where he landed in a moaning heap.

I made a move to run to Mike's side when the Morphosisapien took one stride in my direction and knocked me into a different wall. The pain was excruciating.

"As I was saying," the Morpho said as he casually strode through the room, "My failure with you three has been weighing on my mind. When the two of you made contact with my mind, I knew a day of reckoning was near." He stopped and set his gaze, pointing at each of us as he said, "And I plan on making you suffer."

Pete, who had remained motionless, said, "Why should it bother you so much? We're just three puny humans."

"That's exactly why!" he shouted.

He spoke the words with such power that I felt as if I were experiencing increased g-forces. I could see that both Mike and Pete winced, having similar reactions. The Morpho shifted his focus to Mike, dismissing us entirely. From the sheer confidence radiating off him, it was clear he saw neither Pete nor me as any kind of threat. As he focused his gaze on Mike, Mike struggled heroically to regain his feet.

"You were the strong one as a child as well," it said. "For that reason, I will begin with you, so that your friends will understand the hopelessness of the situation."

He set his sights on the bracelet. I could see lights flashing in rapid succession as the fingers of his right hand manipulated the petal-shaped buttons. When he had completed the task, Mike lay on the floor writhing in pain, his body stiff as a starched collar. His shouts of agony filled the space and bore into my soul.

Pete walked to my side as surreptitiously as possible and quietly said, "We need to get that bracelet."

I nodded, not wanting to gain the Morpho's attention. I peered at Mike and saw the creature kneeling at his side, occasionally poking and prodding his victim.

Whispering, I said to Pete, "We need to get into its head. Are you ready to try?"

Pete nodded, and I threw my arms around him. He immediately reciprocated.

The moment I sensed the Morphosisapien's presence, I shouted in our shared mind, *"Stop!"* Pete immediately echoed the command, and together we tried to seize control. The creature's head whipped toward us, eyes blazing with hatred. But at least Mike's torment ceased under the weight of its attention. I pushed harder, changing the command. Pete and I raised our voices as one in the mind, *"Lie down!"* The beast resisted, every muscle taut with fury, yet slowly it began to comply. I could feel its rage mounting, a storm pressing against us. With every heartbeat, our hold slipped further away.

"We have to do something," I said to Pete. "We're losing control."

"I know. What?"

"Just concentrate," I advised.

We redoubled our efforts, and for a moment, I thought we'd

been successful. Then, steadily, our kidnapper began to exert control.

"No!" I shouted, to no avail.

As the being was regaining control of its body, Pete shouted, "Help! Please!"

It seemed to me to be an empty plea, never to be met. Then I felt multiple surges of energy entering my body. Each caused me to jerk in response, as if being jolted by electricity over and over. I saw Pete having the same experience. Out of the corner of my eye, I saw the Morphosisapien on its knees, about to rise to its full, rage-filled height.

Pete and I disengaged, and I felt a surge of power unlike anything I'd ever experienced. I looked at Pete, and he seemed to have grown taller, with a glow around him, like a visible aura. Based on the look he gave me, it seemed as if I, too, reflected a similar change. The creature rose and, as it was about to unleash a primeval roar, Pete and I clasped hands and shouted.

"No! Get down, now!"

The look of astonishment on its bird-head face as it unwillingly complied would have been comical had it been any other moment.

Pete shouted, "Remove the bracelet and slide it to me!" When it didn't immediately comply, he said, "Now!"

Instantly, the bracelet was slid to Pete, stopping at his feet.

We continued to hold each other with one hand. With his free hand, he picked the bracelet up, affixed it to his left wrist, and worked its flashing petal-shaped controls. He motioned toward the giant being with his head, and I turned to see it prone, invisibly attached to the floor.

"How?" I asked.

Ignoring my question, Pete said, "Follow me," as he made his way to Mike. We both knelt next to Mike's still body. If it hadn't been for the shallow rise and fall of his chest, I would have thought he was gone. Still holding one of my hands, Pete said, "Put your free hand on his heart." I did so as Pete placed his free hand on Mike's head.

We remained in that position without speaking, concentrating on healing our friend. I could feel energy leaving my body and entering Mike's. As the energy transfer continued, I could see Pete's aura fade. I glanced at my body and witnessed the same phenomenon. Steadily, Mike's breathing regained its normal rhythm and, as the last of our auras vanished, Mike opened his eyes and said, "Hey, what's happening?"

Pete and I looked at each other and, laughing, we each placed our heads on Mike's chest.

●●●

When we had regained our composure, I said to Pete, "Care to explain?"

"As best I can," he said. "I'm not really sure how, but the

energy surge we felt was the energy of the previous victims."

I looked around the room, searching for evidence. Finding none, I said, "What?!?"

Pete said, "Wait," and was immediately in contact with the spokesperson. The conversation completed, he said, "They've never tried anything like that before. It was desperation."

Mike, also looking around the room for some manifestation of their existence, said, "Please thank them."

"No need. You can talk directly to them. They just can't answer you, except through me."

Mike and I were helpless to stop looking around the room, as if we could somehow conjure them. Together we said, "Thank you."

"You're welcome," Pete said.

"So, now what?" I asked.

Pete took a moment, consulted, and said, "Because he's mostly created from energy, we're not going to be able to kill him, even if that were an option."

"As much as I'd like to," I said, "I'm not sure I could do it."

Mike remained quiet on the subject.

"So, can we lock the controls and keep him attached to the floor? Maybe send this cube back to another dimension with him like that?"

"That's a possibility, but they are confident he would find a way to escape. There are others of his kind out there who could assist him. If that happened, he'd be sure to come back and exact a terrible revenge. His ancestors were masters at that."

Mike asked, "Can we maroon him somewhere?"

"Same answer," Pete said. He paused to listen before continuing. "There is one thing they suggest that would be more permanent."

"Go on," I said.

"Apparently, we have the ability to create energy, like how we got into this cube. There are different types of energy. One is a binding energy. We could wrap it in this binding energy and place it in stasis while it's wrapped. There's a stasis chamber in this cube."

Mike said, "He said this thing had everything he could need. He wasn't lying."

"OK, what are we waiting for? Mike, you good with that?"

Mike said, "It sounds viable. Let's do it."

"All right. They'll tell me what to do and we'll do it. Follow me."

We walked to where the fallen Morphosisapien lay, still emitting vocal evidence of its struggling. Following Pete's instructions, we stood over it, forming a triangle. We were close enough to one another that we could reach out and hold hands.

Pete slowly punched a series of flashing petal keys on his newly acquired jewelry. As he did, the still body of the Morphosisapien rose, stopping at our chest height.

Pete said, "We'll need to hold hands and tilt our heads forward so our marks are facing each other."

"Our heads don't need to touch?" I asked.

"Nope." Pete answered. "Ready?"

Mike and I nodded. Pete touched a new series of flashing control petals on his bracelet, and the body spun. He reached his hands out, and we did the same, so all of us were in contact, heads leaning forward to expose our markings.

"Think 'binding energy,'" Pete instructed.

We did, and three lines of energy shot forward, one from each of our markings, forming the three-pronged symbol, with the meeting point centered just above the spinning body. Shooting down from that meeting point was a line of concentrated golden energy, like a thread being dispensed from a foot on a sewing machine. As the body spun, the thread moved up and down the body, encasing it in layer after layer, until none of the physical being was visible. A golden energy mummy.

Our hands disengaged, and Pete used the bracelet to lower the body to the floor. The struggles of the Morphosisapien had ceased.

"I'm exhausted," I said.

Pete responded by saying, "Yeah, they said it might do that."

Once again, Pete worked on his bracelet. The body rose and floated to an opening that had appeared in a far wall. In the opening, I saw streams of what could only be energy. Not the golden energy we had produced, but a blue, static, crackling energy. The blue energy embraced the mummy as it floated into the opening, which then seamlessly disappeared.

●●●

Wordlessly, Pete, Mike, and I converged and embraced. We stood like that for minutes, basking in the relief that followed an unexpected victory.

"I can't believe it," I said. "After fifty years, we finally have answers. Let's go home."

"I'll second that motion," Mike said. "Let's go."

Pete remained silent, and both of us sensed that something was not as it should be.

"What?" I said.

"I haven't been totally open with you," he admitted.

We waited.

"In order to keep him in there and wrapped in the binding energy," he said, motioning to where the stasis chamber was, "one of us has to stay here."

"What the fuck are you talking about?" Mike said. "Why?"

"If no creator of the binding energy is near, the binding will weaken over time and eventually fail."

"Did you not think that was an important fact to have mentioned earlier?" Mike said. "What were you thinking?"

"Of course I thought it was important, Mike. That's why I didn't mention it. If I had, the two of you would have fought doing what needed to be done. And don't tell me you wouldn't have, because we all know that would be a lie."

"Are you thinking what I think you're thinking?" I asked.

Pete nodded and said, "I am."

"Why?" Mike asked.

"Because it makes sense for me, and not for either of you. I have no life of my own and haven't since being locked away in that loony bin. Jack, you have a wife and a job, with people who rely on you. Mike, you stop killers, which is one reason you were so valuable to what we did here. You may have retired, but you're not done. You can keep doing it as a consultant. People in our world need you to keep doing what you do. For me, this is the first, and probably last, opportunity I'll ever have to fulfill any type of purpose. My life to this point has been a waste. Let me finally do something that benefits others."

We stared at each other in silence.

"Are you sure?" I asked.

"Jack, I've never been surer of anything in my entire life."

I stepped forward to embrace him, and Mike joined.

"Speaking for both of us, we feel like we just got you back. We're sorry to see you go, but totally understand."

Mike wiped a tear as he nodded in agreement.

Pete held a finger up in the universal "wait a minute" gesture. As he listened to the voice in his head, I could feel disbelief, quickly replaced by loving acceptance.

"Jack, there's something I need to tell you."

I stared at him, puzzled.

"You know the spokesperson I've been talking to?"

"Yes."

"It's Ralphie."

I collapsed to my knees as tears escaped uncontrollably. Sobbing, I croaked out, "Ralphie. Oh my God. Ralphie. I'm so sorry about what happened. I miss you every day."

"Jack, there's nothing for you to be sorry about. What happened, happened. I'm sorry I wasn't able to be there for you as you grew up."

I gaped at Pete and said, "Ralphie, is it really you? How can it be?"

"It is, Jack. I know it's a lot to get your head around, but I promise, it's me. At least as much of 'me' as can be. It's my energy. My essence. Those of us who died here have a little of ourselves left. We've had nothing to do but observe the Morphosisapien, some of us for decades or more. We know how everything in this cube functions. With Pete acting as our physical body, we'll finally have some freedom."

He paused for a moment, and I could see Pete concentrating.

"The others want to thank you for giving us the opportunity to fight back," Ralphie continued. "We didn't even know that was possible."

I stood, walked to Pete/Ralphie, and silently embraced them.

"I've missed you," Ralphie said. "It was terrible having to watch you get stuck in this trap, but I was so proud of your having escaped. I have access to Pete's memories, and I'm glad you've had a good life. Just know that I'm all right. I love you."

"I love you, too, Ralphie. Look after Pete."

# EPILOGUE

Pete let us out of the cube, and Mike and I were standing in the same spot from which we had entered. The sun was going down, but it was still light enough to be considered daytime. Neither of us had any idea how long we'd been gone.

I found my phone still lodged in my pocket and called Anna. She answered while the echo of the ring still reverberated through cyberspace.

"Jack? Jack, is that you?"

"It is," I said. "Can you come get us, please?"

Crying, she said, "Oh my God. Of course, where are you?"

"Same place you dropped us off."

"I'm on my way."

●●●

She threw the transmission into park, jumped out of the car before it had come to a complete rest, and rushed towards us. She embraced me and, after I had joined her, opened her arms to include Mike. Tears flowed freely.

She stepped back, looked around, and said, "Where's Pete?"

I knew this was going to be difficult, but there was no avoiding it.

"Pete stayed behind," I said.

"Stayed behind? Stayed behind where? Is he OK? Are you going to get him?"

I reached for her and said, "Pete's fine. Probably better than he's been since we were ten-years-old. It was his choice."

She was completely confused, looking from me to Mike, and back again.

"Let's go home and we'll explain everything."

She took my hand and said, "All right." As she led us to the car, she said, "You know, until I saw that streak of gold light shoot from your heads and you all disappeared, I was convinced you were all suffering from a shared delusion."

"I know," I replied.

"I'm still not sure what it is I witnessed, but I'm sorry for doubting you."

I chuckled as I said, "I'd have been a little worried if you hadn't."

"By the way," Mike said, "How long have we been gone?"

"Three days," she said. "Three excruciatingly long full days."

"Told you so," I said, laughing.

●●●

We ordered one of those perfect Chicago pizzas, opened a bottle of wine, and Mike and I spent the rest of the night explaining what had happened. The various looks that crossed Anna's face over the course of the evening were priceless. She asked questions, and we answered as best we could.

"I know this all really happened to you, but it's still totally unbelievable. Holy shit!"

"I think that's an accurate, succinct summarization," I replied.

"And Ralphie. Your instincts were right. I'm so glad you got closure on that, too."

"All in all, I'd say this was more successful than we could have possibly hoped. Maybe we even made The Park a safe space once again."

Three glasses came up and met, the clinking sound reverberating unnaturally through the room.

●●●

Mike stayed another couple of days, just visiting and relaxing. One thing he did was to call his brother and speak to him for the first time in years.

He went back to the middle of nowhere, Montana, feeling better about life than he had when he came out.

We continued to stay in contact. No amount of time or distance will ever come between us doing so again.

●●●

Both Anna and I became more relaxed. Having gone through this together had set us at ease, even if we both had to rethink everything we thought we knew about our world and its history. I was looking forward to the next part of this journey.

●●●

About three months after the event, Anna and I were spending a quiet evening at home. We were watching a sci-fi movie and commenting throughout about how much of what we were watching wasn't really fiction. As we watched what was to have been a climactic scene, the screen went dark.

"Are you kidding me?" I moaned as I grabbed the remote and searched for a button that would magically bring the screen to life. Unable to complete the fix, I dropped the remote in disgust.

"Time for a new television?" asked Anna.

"Apparently," I said.

No sooner was the word out of my mouth than the screen came to life. Except it wasn't black. It was a visual cacophony of changing colors.

"That's weird," Anna noted.

"It is," I said, reaching for the remote.

I was about to try a button when the screen came to life.

GREETINGS, PUNY HUMAN EARTHLINGS! DO NOT TRY TO FIX YOUR PRIMITIVE TELEVISION SET. I AM IN CONTROL.

"What the fuck?" was all I could say.

IT IS I, YOUR FRIENDLY INTER-DIMENSIONAL BEST BUD. I HOPE YOU ARE WELL AND THRIVING IN YOUR DIMENSION. I JUST WANTED TO LET YOU KNOW I AM WELL AND HAVE A MESSAGE FOR YOU:

THIS IS FUCKING AWESOME!!!

# POST-EPILOGUE
# ANNA'S FINAL JOURNAL ENTRY

*So much for logic and analysis! How wrong can one person be? Very!*

*Had I not seen the golden stream of light, and the boys' disappearance, with my own eyes, there's nothing that could have made me believe it. Nothing! But I did, and there's no turning back from that.*

*Holy shit! Everything I thought I knew needs to be revisited with a completely altered consciousness.*

*Other dimensions, alien beings, and Pete galivanting around infinite universes accompanied by the energies of long dead "people" from an untold number of species. It's a wonder I've maintained any level of sanity at all.*

*What's next?*

# The End

# ACKNOWLEDGEMENTS

The Park.

It's a real place and, yes, it was the center of my childhood universe. And that of my group of friends, many of whom I am still friends with to this day (see the dedication of this book). Nearly every day began at the Park.

I know it might seem like fiction to some of you, but there was a time, before personal computers, the internet, cell phones, and GPS, that kids had free reign over their neighborhoods. Our bicycles were our tickets to freedom, and we took full advantage. Hence, the way in which this story unfolds is closer to fact than you might imagine.

I have long wanted to write a story centered on the Park. Ideas were tossed around and discarded. Then I remembered how much I enjoyed reading Stephen King's stories. My favorites are not of the horror variety, rather what could be termed his non-horror catalogue. One of those, *The Body*, was turned into a terrific movie, *Stand By Me*. The relationship of the kids in that story always struck a chord with me, probably because of my lifelong friendships. So, I decided to write a story that was an homage to that, centered on the Park. Rather than write pure horror, which is not my forte, I instead choose to go with, for lack of a better label, supernatural fiction. The vehicle for that part of the story is history and the rampant anomalies mainstream archeology chooses to ignore. Who knows, maybe this story is closer to the truth than any of the currently accepted theories. And voila, *A Safe Space* was born.

I hope you enjoyed the read. Feel free to contact me and let me know. My website is Jeffreyjaylevinauthor.com.

As always, I want to thank my wife, Alexis, for her reading, re-reading, and re-re-reading of the manuscript. If there weren't too many typos or mistakes, we have her to thank.

I'd also like to thank Golden Gate/Fawcett Publishing for their hard work and guidance.

Until next time, keep reading.

Peace.

JEFFREY JAY LEVIN
WATCHING
A DIFFERENT TYPE OF TIME TRAVEL
VOLUME I
THE GARDEN MUSEUM HEIST

JEFFREY JAY LEVIN
WATCHING
A DIFFERENT TYPE OF TIME TRAVEL
VOLUME 2
PORTRAIT OF AN INNOCENT GIRL

JEFFREY JAY LEVIN
DEEP
COVER
THE UNKNOWING AGENT

# ABOUT THE AUTHOR

Jeffrey Jay Levin is an award winning author of fiction. He lives in northern Arizona with his wife, Alexis, and has two wonderful daughters and two amazing grandchildren. He has been a restaurant owner, commercial real estate attorney, glass blower, and screenwriter. He is a classic muscle-car enthusiast, rebuilding and remodeling a 1976 Corvette in his "spare" time.

His mind rarely rests, spinning tales he turns into compelling stories. Nothing makes him happier than hearing that a reader really enjoyed his work.

9 798889 795861 0